The Widow Without Hands

Stories From The Channel

R. D. Thorne

Special Thanks, Always:

Cindy, Luca, Leo, Loki
David, Lily, Jaime

Table of Contents

Prologue:

The Curse of Elsbeth Korrin

The mist came to Senčna Vas as it always did—silent, cold, bearing the smell of old water and rotting pine. It crept down from the mountains through the narrow valley, swallowing the timber houses one by one until nothing remained but shadows and the distant sound of the river grinding against stone.

In the cottages, the people drew their shutters and hung fresh rowan branches above their doors. They whispered the old words their grandmothers had taught them, the ones that kept evil from crossing the threshold. They did not speak of where the five elders had gone, or why they had taken torches into Črni Les after sunset.

Some things were better left unspoken.

Deep in the Black Wood, where the trees grew so thick that even noon felt like twilight, five hooded figures stood in a circle. Their torches burned with animal fat and pitch, the flames struggling against the damp air, casting long shadows across ground that had not seen sunlight in a hundred years. The clearing was old, older than the village, older than memory. Moss covered everything like a burial shroud.

At the center, bound to a post of blackened wood, stood Elsbeth Korrin.

She did not weep. She did not beg.

Her hair hung loose around her shoulders, black as a crow's wing, tangled with bits of bark and forest debris from the journey through the trees. Her dress was the same brown wool she wore when she delivered children into the world, when she mixed poultices for the dying, when she sat through long winter nights at the bedsides of the fevered. Now it was torn. Muddied. But her eyes remained steady, moving from one hooded face to the next.

"You know what you do here," she said. Her voice carried no fear. Only a terrible, quiet certainty.

The tallest elder stepped forward. His boots cracked the frozen moss. Elsbeth could not see his face beneath the hood, but she recognized the tremor in his hands as he unrolled the parchment. The paper crackled like breaking ice.

"Elsbeth Korrin," he began. His voice was thick. Wrong. "You are accused—"

"Of what?" Her interruption cut as sharply as a midwife's knife. "Of stopping blood? Of turning breech babies? Of knowing which roots draw out poison and which bark brings down fever?" She looked at each hooded figure in turn. "Twenty years I have served. Twenty years since they buried my husband and left me alone. Twenty years I have come when called, no matter the hour, no matter the cold."

"The crops blackened in the field." A second elder spoke, his voice hard as river stone. "The cattle sicken and fall. Children wake screaming. The river runs foul."

"And so you bring me here?" Elsbeth's laugh was short, bitter. "I am not God. I do not command the wheat or the rain or the river. Nature follows its own path. Sickness comes when it comes. This has always been the way of things."

2

"You were heard speaking to shadows," a third elder whispered, his voice barely carrying across the clearing. "Old Marta saw lights in your window when decent people sleep. You gathered mushrooms beneath the moon."

"I speak to no one but the sick and my cat," Elsbeth said. Weariness was beginning to show at the corners of her mouth. "And yes, the white mushrooms must be cut when the moon is full, or they have no power. This is knowledge. My mother knew it. Her mother before her. It has kept your children alive through winter sickness and summer flux for generations."

But she could see it in their stance, in the set of their shoulders beneath those heavy cloaks—they had not brought her here to listen. They had brought her here to make themselves feel safe again. To give their fear a face. A name. A body to burn.

A fourth elder stepped forward, standing slightly apart from the others. This one was shorter, the movements slower, more careful. The voice, when it came, was older than the rest, dry as autumn leaves.

"You went too far into the dark, Elsbeth Korrin. You opened doors that should remain closed. You disturbed the boundary between this world and the next."

Elsbeth's breath caught. How did they know? The board, The Channel, she had carved it in secret, in the long nights after they buried her husband. It was only meant to comfort her. To let her speak to him one more time. She had told no one. No one.

"I have done nothing wrong," she said, but uncertainty had crept into her voice now.

"You made a thing," the old voice continued. "A tool to reach beyond the veil. To call back what should not be called. This is forbidden knowledge. Dangerous knowledge."

"I only wanted—" Elsbeth stopped. What could she say? That loneliness had driven her to carve symbols into wood by candlelight? That grief had taught her to read the old books, the forbidden ones, hidden in her grandmother's chest? That she had only wanted to hear her husband's voice one more time?

"It does not matter what you wanted," the eldest said. "Only what you did."

The tallest elder, the one who had spoken first, cleared his throat. He would not look at her. His hands shook as he rolled up the parchment. "For the safety of Senčna Vas. For the protection of our children." He paused. Swallowed hard. "You will be cleansed by fire."

The words hung in the mist like a curse themselves.

For the first time, something flickered across Elsbeth's face. Not fear of death—she had sat with enough dying to know it came for everyone. But fear of the injustice. Of being condemned for the very gifts that had kept these people alive.

"Please," she said, and now her voice did break, just slightly. "Do not do this. I have harmed no one. I swear it on my husband's grave. On the graves of every child I have brought safely into this world."

But the elders were already moving. Torches lowered. The kindling around the post had been soaked in rendered fat, causing it to catch quickly. Flames rushed upward, eager and hungry. Smoke rose, thick and black.

Elsbeth coughed. The heat pressed against her skin like hands. Through the smoke and gathering flames, she could see the hooded figures standing in their circle, watching. Witnessing. None of them moved to help her. None of them spoke in her defense.

She understood then, fully, completely, that she would die here. That these people, whom she had served faithfully for twenty years, had decided she was more dangerous alive than dead. That fear and superstition had won.

Something inside Elsbeth cracked.

Not her body. Not yet. But something older. Something that had been passed down through generations of women who knew the herbs and spoke the old words and brought life into the world with bloody hands.

"You want a curse?" Her voice rose above the crackling flames. It no longer sounded entirely human. "Then I will give you one."

The elders stumbled backward. The flames seemed to pause, as if listening.

Elsbeth's voice dropped lower. It came from somewhere deep, from the earth itself, perhaps. From the bones of the mountains.

"I bind this village to my pain! I bind it to the wrong done here. Every generation, when a midwife brings forth new life, my mark will appear. My suffering will be remembered. My spirit will not rest!"

Her hands, gripping the ropes that bound her to the post, were already blackening. The flesh blistered and split. The smell was sweet and terrible, like roasted meat, but wrong.

"I call to the old powers!" The words came faster now. The flames climbed higher, wrapping around her legs, her torso. "I call to the spaces between worlds! To the channels that bridge the living and the dead. Let my spirit walk those boundaries. Let my presence be felt. Let no one forget what was done here this night."

One of the elders made a strangled sound. Another turned away. But none of them moved to stop the flames. None of them called for mercy.

"Let my hands," Elsbeth's voice was raw now, scraped thin by smoke and pain, "these hands that caught babies and healed wounds and eased suffering, let them be remembered. Let them mark this village. Let them appear as a warning and a reminder. Let no midwife forget. Let no mother feel safe while this injustice stands unavenged!"

The flames took her completely then. Her screams tore through the forest, animal sounds, raw and agonized. The elders turned away, one by one. They could not watch. Could not bear witness to what they had done.

But they did not leave. They stood in their circle, hoods drawn low, and waited for the screaming to stop.

It took a long time.

When silence finally fell, it was absolute. The flames continued to burn, consuming what remained, but the forest itself seemed to hold its breath. The mist crept back into the clearing, though the heat should have driven it away. The temperature dropped so quickly that frost formed on the edges of the torches, on the elders' cloaks.

The tallest elder took one step forward, his boots crunching on frozen ground. "Is it finished?"

The answer came not in words.

On the trunk of the oak tree to the north, a black handprint appeared. Perfect. Stark. As if someone had pressed charred fingers against the pale bark.

Then another. On the pine to the south. On the spruce to the east. On the birch to the west.

One by one, they materialized, burned handprints spreading outward from the clearing like a sickness. On stones. On fallen logs. On the frozen ground itself. Each one identical: the print of a woman's hand, fingers splayed, black as soot.

"*Gospod pomiluj*," one of the elders whispered. Lord, have mercy.

But there would be no mercy. The handprints continued spreading, moving through the forest like something alive. The temperature continued falling. The elders' breath came out in white clouds that hung in the air like ghosts.

"We must go," the eldest said, and for the first time, there was fear in that dry voice. Real fear. "We must go now."

They ran.

Not in an orderly fashion, not with the dignity befitting village elders. They fled through the forest like animals, torches forgotten, cloaks snagging on branches. Behind them, the handprints continued to spread, a silent plague moving through Črni Les, marking everything it touched.

By the time they emerged from the forest, the eastern sky was beginning to pale. They stood at the edge of the village, gasping, their faces slick with sweat despite the cold. None of them spoke. None of them looked at the others.

They would tell the villagers that Elsbeth Korrin had been cast out. Shunned for her dark practices. That she had left in the night, cursing their names as she went. But curses were only words. Words could not harm the righteous.

This was the story they agreed upon in silence, standing there in the predawn darkness. This was the lie they would tell their children, and their children's children. The truth would remain locked in their hearts, five people who knew what had really happened in the clearing, who had watched an innocent woman burn.

For just that morning, the elders had brought Elsbeth before the village, where the accusations of another midwife, Lillith, against Elsbeth rang out for all to hear. Hastily and without mercy, they had pronounced their judgment: exile. The villagers had watched, satisfied that justice was being served, as the elders led Elsbeth away.

But exile was a lie.

The elders did not take her to the edge of the village and release her. They did not point her toward distant cities and warn her never to return.

Instead, they took her deep into Črni Les, where no villager would follow, where no witness would see.

But in Črni Les, in that hidden clearing where nothing would ever grow again, the marks remained. The post—nothing more than a charred stick, all but consumed by fire—was surrounded by a perfect circle of black handprints pressed into the earth like a scar.

And as years passed and seasons turned, the marks would sometimes reappear, a black handprint on a doorframe, on a cradle, on a midwife's wall, reminding the village that some curses are not mere words.

Some curses are promises kept.

Deep in the forest, buried beneath decades of leaf-fall and new growth, lay the object Elsbeth had carved during the empty nights after her husband died. A board of dark wood, marked with symbols and letters from the old alphabet. Designed to bridge the gap between the living and the dead. A tool for speaking to spirits. For channeling them.

She had called it The Channel.

It had been her comfort. Her secret. Her way of reaching across the veil to speak once more with the man she loved. An innocent thing, born of grief and loneliness.

But in her final moments, as the flames consumed her body and her spirit tore free, Elsbeth had bound herself to it. The Channel had become something more than a tool. It had become a doorway. A bridge. An anchor that would hold her restless spirit to the world she had left behind.

The elders never found it.

But it waited there, patient as stone, for the day when another woman with healing hands and a child to protect would need to speak with the dead. It waited for someone brave enough to listen to a ghost's story. To uncover the truth buried beneath generations of lies.

The curse of Elsbeth Korrin had begun. It would not end until justice was served or vengeance taken—or both.

Chapter 1:

The Marked Cradle

The cottage was quiet except for the creak of the rocking chair and the soft sound of Lila breathing. Briony held her daughter close, feeling the weight of her, small and warm and alive, against her chest. The baby's eyes were half-closed, her tiny fist curled against Briony's worn dress. Outside, the mist was settling over Senčna Vas, turning everything gray and distant.

Briony sang an old lullaby, one her own mother had sung before the fever took her. The melody was simple, the words in the old tongue, about a bird finding its way home through the forest. Lila's breathing began to slow, deepen. Her small body grew heavier with sleep.

Duska, Briony's cat, sat at her feet, his tail curled around his paws. In the dim light of the cottage, his gray fur looked almost black. He watched the baby with unblinking yellow eyes, patient and still as a shadow.

The fire in the hearth had burned down to embers. Briony would need to add more wood soon, but not yet. Not while Lila was finally settling. The baby had been fussy all day, crying for reasons Briony could not determine. No fever. No sign of colic. Just an unsettled restlessness that had kept them both awake since dawn.

Briony looked around the cottage, her cottage, though it had belonged to the midwife before her, and the one before that. It was small: one main room with the hearth, a table, two chairs, and bundles of dried herbs hanging from the low ceiling. Lavender and sage, yarrow and chamomile, their scents mixing with the smell of wood smoke and old stone. A narrow doorway led to the back room where Briony slept, where Lila's cradle sat beside the bed.

The cradle had been carved by Briony's grandfather, back when her mother was born. It was made of dark wood, worn smooth by generations of babies. Briony had lined it with soft wool and linen, the best she could afford. She had hung small charms around it, elderberries threaded on string, a sprig of rowan, a small bag of salt sewn into cloth. Old protections. The kind her grandmother had taught her.

The kind that were supposed to keep evil away.

Lila's eyes finally closed completely. Her breathing fell into the deep rhythm of true sleep. Briony waited another moment, then slowly rose from the rocking chair. The floorboards creaked beneath her feet—they always did, no matter how carefully she stepped. Duska stood as well, stretching before padding after her toward the back room.

The light was dimmer here. Briony had lit only one candle, and it cast long shadows across the walls. She moved toward the cradle, holding Lila carefully, preparing to lay her down.

Then she saw it.

On the wall beside the cradle, just above where Lila's head would rest, was a handprint.

Briony stopped. Her breath caught in her throat.

The print was black, not the brown of mud or the gray of ash, but black as soot, as char, as something burned beyond recognition. It was the size of a woman's hand, fingers splayed wide, pressed against the whitewashed wall as if someone had reached out to steady themselves.

But no one had been in this room except Briony. No one had touched that wall.

A cold shiver ran down Briony's spine, settling in her stomach like a stone. She knew what this was. Everyone in Senčna Vas knew the stories, even if they did not speak of them openly. The black handprints. The mark of Elsbeth Korrin. The sign that the old curse was stirring again.

Briony had heard the tales since she was a child. How Elsbeth had been cast out, or shunned, or had simply left, depending on who told the story, centuries ago. How she had cursed the village as she departed. How sometimes, when misfortune came, black handprints would appear. On doorframes. On walls. On the sides of wells.

Always black. Always the shape of a woman's hand.

But Briony had never seen one herself. They were stories. Warnings. Things that happened long ago, in her grandmother's time, or her grandmother's grandmother's time.

Not now. Not here. Not in her home.

Lila stirred in her arms, making a small sound of protest. Briony realized she was holding her too tightly. She forced herself to breathe, to loosen her grip, to move. Carefully, she laid Lila in the cradle, tucking the soft blanket around her small body. The baby settled immediately, her face relaxing into sleep.

Duska jumped onto the bed and sat at the edge, staring at the handprint. His ears were flat against his head. The tip of his tail twitched once, twice.

Briony stepped closer to the wall. In the candlelight, the print seemed to shimmer slightly, as if it were not quite dry.

But when she reached out, her hand trembling, and touched it, the wall was cold and completely dry. The black mark did not smudge or transfer to her fingers. It was as if it had been burned into the very plaster.

Why? The question rose in her mind like a scream. Why would the curse mark her? She was no one. Just an apprentice midwife, still learning the craft from Ana. Just a girl who had made a mistake, who had trusted the wrong man, who now had a baby and no husband and a future that looked darker with each passing day.

She thought of the stories again, trying to remember the details. The handprints appeared when the curse was active, that much she knew. But what made it active? What woke it from its long sleep?

She could not remember. The stories were always vague, told in whispers, full of warnings but short on details. The elders knew more, probably. They always did. But they did not share their knowledge freely, especially not with someone like Briony.

Someone like her. An outsider, even though she had been born in this village.

It had not always been this way. Before Lila, Briony had been simply the girl training to be a midwife. People had been wary of her—they were always wary of midwives, those women who dealt with blood and birth and the thin line between life and death—but they had not shunned her. They had nodded to her in the village square. Had called her when their wives went into labor. Had paid her in bread and eggs and small copper coins.

Then she had started to show.

It had been winter when she realized she was pregnant. The trader, his name was Andrej, though she tried not to think of him anymore, had been gone for two months by then. He had come to Senčna Vas in late summer, selling fabric and ribbons and small luxuries from the cities to the west. He had been charming. Handsome. He had smiled at Briony in the market square and asked her name.

She had been so lonely.

Her mother was five years dead. Her father had died when she was too young to remember him. She had no siblings. Only Ana, her mentor, and Ana's husband, Marko, treated her with real kindness. Everyone else kept their distance, as they always did with midwives.

So when Andrej had paid attention to her, when he had sought her out, when he had whispered that she was beautiful and special and different from the other girls, she had believed him.

It had only been a few times. Secret meetings in the forest, away from the village's watching eyes. He had promised he would return, that he would take her with him next time, that they would have a life together in one of the big cities where no one cared about superstitions and old curses.

Then he had left. And he had not come back.

By midwinter, when Briony could no longer hide the swell of her belly beneath her shawls, the village had turned cold. Women pulled their children away from her in the street. Men would not meet her eyes. Ana had been kind, had delivered Lila when the time came, had told Briony she was strong and brave, and that the baby was healthy.

But even Ana could not protect her from the whispers. From the looks. From the way people now crossed to the other side of the street when they saw her coming.

An unmarried mother. An apprentice midwife who should have known better. A girl who consorted with outsiders and then tried to raise a child alone, as if that were something decent people did.

And the cat did not help. Briony had found Duska as a tiny kitten, abandoned near the river, mewing pitifully. She had taken him in, fed him, let him sleep by her fire. He had grown into a large, sturdy cat with gray fur that could look black in dim light. Black cats were unlucky. Everyone knew that. They were associated with witches, with dark magic, with things that should not be spoken of.

Briony knew what people said about her. That she was following in Elsbeth's footsteps. That midwives always walked too close to the darkness. That it was only a matter of time before she brought real misfortune to the village.

And now this. A black handprint on her wall. The curse, marking her home. Marking her baby.

Briony looked down at Lila, sleeping so peacefully in her cradle, unaware of the danger. Unaware of anything except warmth and milk and the sound of her mother's heartbeat. She was so small. So helpless. So entirely dependent on Briony to keep her safe.

"I will protect you," Briony whispered. "No matter what. I promise."

Duska made a low sound in his throat, not quite a growl, not quite a meow. His eyes were still fixed on the handprint.

Briony realized she was exhausted. The day had been long, Lila had been fussy, and now this. She needed to sleep. Needed to think clearly. In the morning, she would decide what to do. Perhaps she would go to Ana. Ana would know what this meant. Ana always knew.

She changed into her nightdress, the rough linen cold against her skin. The cottage was growing colder as the fire died. She should add more wood, but she was too tired. Tomorrow. Everything could wait until tomorrow.

She climbed into bed, pulling the wool blanket up to her chin. Duska settled beside her, his warm body pressed against her side. From the cradle, she could hear Lila's soft breathing, steady and peaceful.

But Briony could not stop looking at the handprint. Even in the darkness, with only the faint glow of embers from the main room, she could see it. A darker shadow against the wall. Watching. Waiting.

She closed her eyes and tried to sleep.

It took a long time.

When she finally drifted off, her dreams were troubled. She saw forests burning. Women screaming. Black handprints spreading across walls like mold, like disease, like something alive and hungry. She heard a voice calling her name, but when she turned to see who it was, there was only smoke and darkness.

She woke with a start.

Gray dawn light was filtering through the small window. Lila was beginning to stir, making the small sounds that meant she would wake soon and want to be fed. Duska was sitting on the windowsill, his tail swishing slowly back and forth.

Briony sat up, her heart pounding. For a moment, she wondered if the handprint had been part of the dream. A nightmare brought on by exhaustion and stress.

Then she turned and looked at the wall.

There were two handprints now.

The first was still there, exactly where it had been. But now, just below it and slightly to the right, closer to the cradle, was a second print. The same size. The same soot-black color. The fingers reaching toward where Lila slept.

Briony's breath stopped in her chest.

She threw back the blanket and crossed to the cradle in two steps. Lila was fine, stirring but still asleep, her small face peaceful. Briony scooped her up, holding her tight against her chest, feeling the reassuring warmth of her, the realness of her.

The handprints were on the wall. Just marks. They could not hurt anyone.

But even as she thought it, Briony knew it was not true. The marks were not just marks. They were a message. A warning. A sign that something, someone was reaching for her daughter.

The curse was no longer a story from the past. It was here. It was real. It was happening.

And it had chosen Briony and Lila.

Duska jumped down from the window and rubbed against Briony's legs, his purr loud in the quiet room. She looked down at him, then at the baby in her arms, then back at the two black handprints on the wall.

Fear moved through her like cold water. But beneath the fear was something else. Something harder. Stronger.

She was Lila's mother. She was an apprentice midwife, learning to bring life into the world and fight death back when she could. She had survived losing her parents, survived betrayal, survived the village's judgment and scorn. She had brought Lila into the world alone, had kept her alive and healthy despite having so little.

She would not let some ancient curse take her daughter.

"I will not let you have her," Briony said to the empty room, to the handprints, to whatever spirit or force had put them there. Her voice was steady. Certain. "Do you hear me? You cannot have her."

The handprints did not answer. But somehow, standing there in the gray morning light with her daughter in her arms, Briony felt as though her words had been heard.

Lila began to fuss in earnest now, her small mouth seeking, her hands waving. She needed to be fed. She needed to be changed. She needed all the ordinary things that babies need, curse or no curse.

Briony carried her to the bed and began to nurse her, settling against the pillows. Duska jumped up and curled beside them, a warm presence. Outside, Senčna Vas was waking. Soon there would be smoke from chimneys, voices in the street, the normal sounds of morning.

But nothing felt normal anymore.

Briony looked at the handprints again. Two now. Would there be three tomorrow? Four? How many before something worse happened? She needed answers. She needed help. She needed to understand what this curse was and why it had marked her home.

And there was only one person who might be able to tell her. Ana. The next day, Briony would bundle Lila up and go to Ana's house. Ana would know what to do. Ana had to know. Because Briony's fight to save her family had just begun, and she could not do it alone.

Chapter 2:

Shadows of the Past

Briony woke the next morning to pale sunlight filtering through the cottage windows and the sound of Lila stirring in her cradle. For a moment, one blessed, fleeting moment, she felt almost normal. The warmth of her bed, the familiar creaks of the old cottage settling around her, the soft cooing of her daughter... It was enough to make her believe that yesterday had been nothing more than a nightmare.

Then she remembered the handprints.

Briony sat up slowly, her heart already beginning to race. She didn't want to look, didn't want to turn her head toward the corner where Lila's cradle sat bathed in morning light. But she had to know. She had to see if more had appeared during the night.

With a deep breath, she forced herself to look.

The two handprints were still there, the first one high on the wall above the cradle, the second one lower and closer, as if reaching down toward her sleeping daughter. In the daylight, they looked even more unnatural, the soot-black marks standing out starkly against the whitewashed plaster. They seemed to absorb the light rather than reflect it, creating dark voids on the wall that made Briony's stomach turn.

No new ones, at least. Not yet.

Lila let out a small cry, and Briony pushed aside her fear and went to her daughter. She lifted the baby into her arms, holding her close and breathing in that sweet, clean scent that only infants seemed to have. Lila's tiny fist closed around a strand of Briony's red hair, and despite everything, Briony smiled.

"Good morning, little one," she whispered. "We're going on a trip today. We're going to see Ana."

Duska appeared at her feet, winding himself around her ankles and purring loudly. The cat had refused to enter the room last night, but this morning he seemed less agitated, though his green eyes still flicked occasionally toward the handprints on the wall.

Briony dressed quickly and efficiently, pulling on her warmest dress and wrapping Lila in layers of soft cloth and a knitted shawl. She filled a satchel with essentials—clean rags for Lila, a spare dress, some dried herbs she kept for emergencies. She didn't know how long she'd be gone, and she wasn't taking any chances.

As she prepared to leave, Briony paused at the doorway and looked back at the cottage. This place had been her mother's before her, and her grandmother's before that. It had been passed down through generations of midwives, each woman adding her own protections and charms to keep the darkness at bay. The bundles of sage and rowan hung from the rafters, the horseshoes nailed above the doors, the salt laid across the thresholds—all of it was supposed to keep them safe.

But it hadn't worked. The handprints had appeared anyway.

Briony stepped outside and closed the door firmly behind her, Duska darting out ahead of her. The morning air was crisp and cool, carrying the scent of pine and damp earth. Mist clung to the ground in wispy patches, and the forest that surrounded her cottage seemed darker than usual, the trees pressing close as if leaning in to listen.

She walked quickly along the narrow path that led from her cottage toward the village proper, Lila bundled against her chest, Duska trotting at her heels. The village was just beginning to wake; she could see smoke rising from chimneys in the distance, could hear the faint sounds of animals being let out to graze.

As she passed through the outskirts of Senčna Vas, Briony noticed two men standing near the well in the small square, their voices low but urgent. She recognized them both, Jozef, a shepherd she'd known since childhood, and another man whose name she couldn't quite remember. They didn't see her at first, and she caught fragments of their conversation as she drew closer.

"...found three more sheep dead this morning," Jozef was saying, his voice heavy with exhaustion. "Throats torn, but there's no blood. No tracks either. Whatever did this, it wasn't natural."

"My wife's been saying the crops are failing too," the other man replied. "The wheat's turning black on the stalks, and the vegetables in our garden are rotting before they're ripe. And have you heard about the river? They're saying the water's tainted. Old Pavel's livestock drank from it yesterday, and half of them are sick now."

"It's the curse," Jozef said quietly. "Has to be. Just like the old stories."

Briony's breath caught. She wanted to stop, to ask them what they meant, but something told her it would be better to remain unnoticed. She ducked her head and hurried past, keeping to the shadows of the buildings.

The men didn't see her, too absorbed in their worried conversation. But Briony's mind was racing. Dead sheep. Failing crops. Tainted water. These were the signs the old stories spoke of, the signs that Elsbeth's curse was active, spreading its poison through the village like a sickness.

And it had started the same night the first handprint appeared in her cottage.

The realization hit her like a physical blow, and she had to stop walking for a moment to steady herself. This wasn't just about her and Lila. The entire village was suffering because of the curse, because of the handprints that had appeared above her daughter's cradle. Somehow, she and Lila were at the center of this.

But why? What had they done to deserve this?

Briony forced herself to keep moving, walking faster now, her arms tightening protectively around Lila. Ana's house was on the far side of the village, nestled at the edge of a small meadow that backed up against the forest. It was a journey of about twenty minutes at a steady pace, and Briony used every second of it to try to calm the panic that was threatening to overwhelm her.

By the time she reached Ana's door, her heart was pounding, and her hands were shaking. She knocked urgently, glancing over her shoulder as if expecting to see something following her from the village.

The door opened almost immediately, and Ana's familiar face appeared, her expression shifting from curiosity to concern in an instant.

"Briony?" Ana's eyes took in the sight before her, the pale, frightened young woman clutching her baby, the dark-furred cat at her feet, the barely concealed terror in Briony's eyes. "What's happened? Come in, quickly."

Briony stumbled inside, and Ana shut the door firmly behind her. The interior of Ana's house was warm and fragrant, filled with the comforting scents of dried herbs, burning candles, and the faint sweetness of essential oils. Bundles of lavender, sage, and rosemary hung from the ceiling beams, and shelves lined the walls, crowded with jars of various sizes containing powders, tinctures, and dried plants.

Marko appeared from the back room, wiping his hands on a cloth. He was a solid, practical man with kind eyes and strong hands, a carpenter by trade, and as steady and reliable as the houses he built.

"Is everything alright?" he asked, his voice low and calm.

Ana gently took Lila from Briony's arms and passed the baby to Marko, who cradled her with the ease of someone who had helped raise many children. Ana then guided Briony to a chair by the fire.

"Sit," Ana said softly. "Take a breath. You're safe here."

Briony sank into the chair, her body trembling with exhaustion and fear. She tried to speak, but her throat felt tight and the words wouldn't come. Ana knelt beside her, taking her hands in a firm, warm grip.

"Start from the beginning," Ana said. "Tell me everything."

And so Briony did. She told them about the first handprint appearing above Lila's cradle, about the cold shiver that had run through her when she saw it. She told them about lying awake at night, watching the cradle, terrified that something would come for her daughter. She told them about waking yesterday to find a second handprint, closer than the first. And she told them about the conversation she'd overheard in the village, the dead sheep, the failing crops, the tainted water.

"They said it was the curse," Briony finished, her voice barely above a whisper. "Elsbeth's curse. And I think they're right. I think it's all connected to the handprints in my cottage. But I don't understand why. What did I do? What did Lila do?"

Ana was silent for a long moment, her expression troubled. She glanced at Marko, who was rocking Lila gently, then back at Briony.

"Come with me," Ana said finally, standing and helping Briony to her feet. "There's something I need to show you. Something I need to tell you. And it's better if we speak in the garden."

Briony followed Ana through the house and out the back door, Duska padding along behind them. Marko stayed inside with Lila, his low voice murmuring soft words to the baby.

Ana's garden was like stepping into another world. It was a place of peace and life, a stark contrast to the fear and death that seemed to be spreading through the village. The garden was filled with rows of herbs, lavender and chamomile swaying in the slight breeze, patches of sage and mint and rosemary growing in wild, fragrant profusion. There were flowerbeds too, spilling over with bright colors, violets and calendula and sunflowers turning their faces toward the sun.

Chickens wandered freely among the plants, pecking at bugs and scratching in the dirt. And there, lounging on a sun-warmed stone, was Oli, Ana's tabby cat, who opened one lazy eye to regard Duska before going back to sleep.

Ana led Briony to a wooden bench beneath an old apple tree, and they sat down together. The morning sun was warm on Briony's face, and for a moment she could almost believe that everything was normal, that the world wasn't falling apart around her.

But then Ana spoke, and the illusion shattered.

"What do you know about Elsbeth Korrin?" Ana asked gently.

Briony frowned, thinking back to the stories she'd heard growing up. "She was a midwife, a long time ago. The villagers accused her of being a witch. They said she brought bad luck, that she cursed the village before she left, or was driven out. The handprints are supposed to be her mark."

Ana nodded slowly. "That's the story the village tells. But it's not the truth. At least, not all of it."

Briony felt a chill run down her spine despite the warmth of the sun. "What do you mean?"

Ana took a deep breath, her hands folding together in her lap. "Elsbeth Korrin was indeed a midwife, and she was kind and skilled. She saved many lives, mothers and babies both. She knew which herbs could stop bleeding, which roots could draw out poison, which bark could bring down a fever. She was beloved in the village, trusted by everyone."

"But then things went wrong," Ana continued, her voice growing heavy with sorrow. "There was a famine one year, and then illness came. Crops failed. Livestock died. Children fell sick. The villagers were terrified, and in their fear, they looked for someone to blame. And they chose Elsbeth."

"Why?" Briony asked, though she thought she already knew the answer.

Ana took a deep breath, her hands folding together in her lap. "The elders came for her and brought her before the village in the square. Lillith, another midwife, older, respected, she accused Elsbeth of witchcraft. She showed them evidence: a carved board with symbols, things that looked dark and forbidden. The villagers were terrified. They believed Lillith."

"What did they do?" Briony asked, though dread was already pooling in her stomach.

"The elders pronounced judgment," Ana said quietly. "They told the village Elsbeth would be cast out, exiled into the wilderness. The villagers watched as they led her away, and they believed she was simply being banished from Senčna Vas."

Ana's voice dropped to barely a whisper. "But that was a lie. The elders didn't exile her. They took her deep into Črni Les, into the Black Wood, where no one would see. And there, with only the five of them as witnesses, they burned her alive."

Briony felt her stomach turn. "The village doesn't know? They think she was just exiled?"

"For three hundred years, that's what they've believed," Ana confirmed. "The elders told them Elsbeth cursed the village as she left, that her evil words caused the marks to appear. But the truth is darker: She cursed them as she burned. She cursed the men who murdered her in secret and the village that believed their lies. The confession you seek will be from one of those elders, written in guilt before he died. It's proof of the murder the village never knew happened."

"How do you know this?" Briony whispered.

Ana's expression grew even more troubled. "Because I am connected to those elders. My great-great-great-grandmother was the sister of one of them. The truth has been passed down through my family, kept secret because of the shame. We've carried that knowledge like a burden, knowing what our ancestors did and being powerless to change it."

She reached out and took Briony's hand. "And there's something else you need to know. When Elsbeth burned, her hands were the first to catch fire. They say she raised them up, even as the flames consumed her, and she cursed the village with her dying breath. Her hands were burned black, down to the bone and ash. And those blackened hands became the symbol of her curse, the mark she left behind."

Briony felt tears burning in her eyes. "The handprints in my cottage."

"Yes," Ana said softly. "The soot-black handprints are said to be Elsbeth's hands reaching from beyond death, marking those who are connected to what was done to her. And midwives... midwives have always been the focus of that mark. Because Elsbeth was a midwife, and her death was the death of a healer. The curse seeks out those who share her calling."

"But why now?" Briony asked, her voice breaking. "Why me? Why Lila?"

Ana squeezed her hand. "I don't know for certain. But I know that midwives in this village have lived under the shadow of that curse for generations. Some have seen the handprints. Some have fled. Some have... not survived. The curse seems to come in waves, appearing every few decades, and it always targets midwives, especially those with children."

Briony's breath came faster. "So Lila is in danger because of me. Because I'm an apprentice midwife."

"No," Ana said firmly. "Lila is in danger because of an injustice that happened long before you were born. Because frightened men chose violence over truth. This is not your fault, Briony. None of this is your fault."

But Briony barely heard her. Her mind was reeling, trying to process everything she'd just learned. Elsbeth had been innocent. She'd been murdered. And her curse had been haunting midwives ever since, passing down through generations like a disease.

"What am I supposed to do?" Briony asked, tears spilling down her cheeks. "How do I protect Lila? How do I stop this?"

Ana was quiet for a long moment. Then she spoke, her words careful and measured. "I don't have all the answers. But I know this: Curses are born from pain and injustice. They feed on secrets and lies. If there's any hope of breaking Elsbeth's curse, you need to uncover the truth, every piece of it. To break the curse, you must bring the truth into the open."

"But how?" Briony pressed. "Where would I even start?"

Ana looked toward the forest in the distance, toward the dark line of trees that marked the edge of Črni Les. "There may be a way. But it's dangerous, and I can't promise it will work. You would need to go into the forest, to the place where Elsbeth died. There may be... something there. Something that could help you understand what Elsbeth wants, what would allow her spirit to rest."

Briony followed her gaze, staring at the dark forest. Fear coiled in her stomach, but beneath it was something stronger—determination. She would do whatever it took to protect Lila. Even if it meant facing the curse directly.

"I'll go," she said quietly.

Ana turned to her, concern written across her face. "Not today. You're exhausted, and you need to think this through. Stay here with us. Rest. Let Marko and me watch over Lila while you gather your strength. And when you're ready, if you're certain this is what you need to do, I'll tell you how to find the place."

Briony wanted to argue, wanted to say that she needed to go now, immediately, before anything else could happen. But Ana was right, she was exhausted, physically and emotionally. And Lila needed her to be strong, to be clearheaded.

"Alright," she said finally. "I'll stay. But only for today."

Ana nodded, relief flickering across her features. "Good. Come, let's go back inside. Marko will have lunch ready soon, and you need to eat. And Lila probably needs feeding too."

They stood and walked back toward the house together, leaving the peaceful garden behind. But as Briony glanced back over her shoulder one last time, her eyes were drawn once more to the dark line of Črni Les on the horizon.

Tomorrow, she would go into that forest. Tomorrow, she would begin searching for answers.

And whatever she found there, whether it was salvation or something far darker, she would face it for Lila's sake.

For all their sakes.

Chapter 3:

Into Črni Les

Briony returned to her cottage as the afternoon sun began its slow descent toward the horizon, painting the sky in shades of amber and rose. Ana had insisted that she take Lila home for the evening, promising that tomorrow they would begin making plans to deal with the curse. But as Briony walked the familiar path from Ana's house back to her own, her mind was anything but calm.

Everything Ana had told her churned through her thoughts like a storm—Elsbeth's murder, the burned hands, the curse that had haunted midwives for generations. And now that curse had found her. It had marked her cottage, marked her baby, and was slowly tightening its grip on both of them.

When Briony reached her cottage, she paused at the door, suddenly afraid of what she might find inside. Would there be more handprints? Would the two that were already there have moved, grown, multiplied?

She took a deep breath, shifted Lila in her arms, and pushed open the door.

The cottage was exactly as she'd left it that morning. The two black handprints were still on the wall by Lila's cradle, one high, one low, but they hadn't changed. They hadn't moved. The sight should have been reassuring, but instead it felt ominous, like the calm before a storm.

Duska slipped inside ahead of her, moving cautiously through the rooms as if checking for danger. The cat paused at the threshold of the bedroom where the handprints were, his ears flattening against his head, but he didn't run away this time. He simply sat down and watched the marks warily.

Briony fed Lila, changed her, and rocked her to sleep as the light outside faded to dusk. She laid her daughter in the cradle, carefully avoiding looking at the handprints on the wall above. But even as she turned away, she could feel their presence, cold and waiting.

She couldn't stay here. Not tonight. Not with her mind so full of fear and questions and terrible knowledge. She needed to think, to process everything she'd learned. She needed clarity.

And she knew where to find it.

Ana had mentioned Črni Les, the Black Wood, when she'd told the story of Elsbeth's execution. The forest where the elders had taken Elsbeth to die. The place where the curse had been born.

Briony had been avoiding that forest her entire life. Everyone in the village avoided it. The Black Wood was a place of dark legends, a place where people said the boundary between the living world and the spirit world grew thin. Children were warned never to go there. Adults crossed themselves when they passed near it.

But if Briony was going to understand this curse, if she was going to find a way to break it and protect Lila, she needed to face it directly. She needed to go to the source.

The decision crystallized in her mind with sudden certainty. She would go to Črni Les. Tonight. While Lila slept peacefully, while the cottage was quiet and still. She would go into the forest and seek the clarity that eluded her here.

She checked on Lila one more time; the baby was sleeping deeply, her tiny chest rising and falling in a steady rhythm. Briony tucked the blankets around her daughter more snugly, whispered a prayer of protection, and then pulled on her warmest cloak.

Duska appeared at her feet, meowing insistently.

"You want to come?" Briony asked softly.

The cat meowed again, more urgently, and moved toward the door.

"Alright. But stay close to me. I don't know what we'll find out there."

And so, with her heart pounding and her hands shaking slightly, Briony stepped out into the gathering darkness with Duska at her heels.

The path to Črni Les was one Briony knew well, though she'd never had the courage to actually enter the forest before. She'd walked past it countless times. It bordered the eastern edge of the village, a dark wall of ancient trees that seemed to lean inward, blocking out the light.

As she approached the tree line, the temperature dropped noticeably. The air grew heavy and damp, carrying the scent of moss and decay and something else, something older and harder to name. The sounds of the village behind her, distant voices, the bark of a dog, the creak of a cart, faded away until there was only silence.

Briony stopped at the edge of the forest and looked up at the towering trees. They were old, older than the village, older than memory. Their trunks were thick and gnarled, their branches twisted into shapes that looked almost deliberate, almost purposeful. In the fading light, they cast long shadows that stretched across the ground like grasping fingers.

Duska pressed against her leg, his body tense but his green eyes fixed on the darkness ahead.

"I know," Briony whispered. "I'm afraid too. But we have to do this."

She took a deep breath and stepped across the threshold into Črni Les.

The change was immediate and profound. The moment her foot touched the forest floor, the world around her seemed to shift. The last remnants of twilight vanished, replaced by a deep, pervasive gloom. The air grew colder still, cold enough that Briony could see her breath misting before her face. And the silence. The silence was absolute, as if the forest had swallowed all sound and refused to give it back.

Briony's footsteps made no noise on the thick carpet of moss and fallen leaves. Even her breathing seemed muffled, absorbed by the oppressive quiet. Duska moved like a ghost beside her, his dark form barely visible in the shadows.

She had no clear destination in mind—Ana hadn't given her specific directions to the place where Elsbeth had died. But something inside Briony seemed to know the way. It was as if the forest itself was guiding her, pulling her deeper into its shadowed heart.

She walked for what might have been minutes or might have been hours. Time felt strange here, stretched and distorted, as if the normal rules that governed the outside world didn't apply within these ancient boundaries. The trees pressed close on either side, their trunks massive and twisted with age, their bark rough and covered with strange patterns that almost looked like faces if she stared at them too long. Their branches reached overhead to form a canopy so thick that no starlight could penetrate, creating a darkness so complete that Briony could barely see more than a few feet ahead.

The only light came from the faint glow of bioluminescent fungi growing on some of the tree trunks, pale blue-green patches that pulsed softly, like the beating of a slow heart. The light they cast was just enough to see by, but it made the forest look even more otherworldly, even more alien. Shadows moved strangely in that dim glow, seeming to shift and change when Briony wasn't looking directly at them.

Briony's rational mind told her to turn back, to flee this place before something terrible happened. But something deeper, some instinct or intuition, drove her forward. She had come here seeking clarity, seeking understanding, and she would not turn back until she found it.

Then, without warning, the trees opened up before her.

Briony stepped into a clearing and stopped, her breath catching in her throat.

It was a perfect circle, perhaps thirty feet across, ringed by tall, bare trees that stood like silent witnesses. Their branches reached upward toward the sky, stripped of all leaves, creating skeletal silhouettes against the dark. The ground within the circle was different from the rest of the forest. Instead of moss and undergrowth, it was covered in a fine layer of gray ash that looked almost like snow in the dim light.

Nothing grew here. No grass, no flowers, no mushrooms or ferns. Just ash and bare earth.

And in the center of the clearing stood the remains of a wooden post.

Briony moved forward slowly, as if in a trance. She could feel the weight of this place pressing down on her, could sense the terrible history that had unfolded here. This was where Elsbeth had died. This was where she had been tied to that post and burned alive while the elders watched. This was where the curse had been born.

The air in the clearing was even colder than the forest around it, so cold that Briony's teeth began to chatter. The ash crunched softly beneath her boots as she walked toward the post. Up close, she could see that it was charred black, its surface cracked and splintered. The wood was ancient, weathered by centuries of wind and rain, but it still stood, a monument to injustice, to murder, to pain.

Briony reached out and touched the post with trembling fingers. The wood was ice-cold, and the moment her skin made contact, a jolt of something—energy, memory, emotion—ran through her body. For a brief instant, she could almost hear screaming, could almost smell smoke and burning flesh, could almost feel the terrible heat of flames.

She jerked her hand back, gasping.

"I'm sorry," she whispered to the empty clearing, to the ghost of the woman who had died here. "I'm so, so sorry for what they did to you."

Duska meowed softly from the edge of the clearing, and Briony turned to look at him. The cat was staring at something on the ground near the base of the post, his tail low and his body tense.

Briony knelt down to see what had caught his attention.

There, partially buried in the ash, was something dark and rectangular. She brushed away the fine gray powder carefully, revealing a piece of wood, a board of some kind, aged and blackened.

Her heart began to race. She cleared away more ash, uncovering more of the object, until finally she could see what it was.

A board, about two feet long and eighteen inches wide, made of dark wood that looked almost black with age. Its surface was covered with strange symbols and letters, some carefully carved, others burned into the grain. At the center was a circle divided into sections, each section holding a unique symbol: a moon, a flame, a spiral, a key, and others she didn't recognize. Around the edge of the board were letters, forming what looked like an alphabet, though not in any order Briony recognized.

And resting in the center of the board was a heart-shaped piece of wood, smooth and worn, small enough to fit in the palm of her hand.

Briony had heard of such things in stories told by the village elders, tools used by those who claimed to speak with spirits. Devices for communication between the living and the dead. Ana had mentioned it briefly when telling Elsbeth's story: The Channel.

This was it. This was the relic Ana had spoken of. The tool Elsbeth had used, the thing the elders had feared and condemned.

With trembling hands, Briony reached down and tried to lift the board from its resting place.

It wouldn't move.

She pulled harder, gripping the edges with both hands, but the board remained fixed in place as if it weighed a thousand pounds. Or as if something, some invisible force, was holding it down, anchoring it to this spot where Elsbeth had died.

Briony sat back on her heels, staring at the board in wonder and fear. The Channel was real. It was here, in this clearing, waiting. But it wouldn't let her take it. It belonged here, in this place of death and curse.

But that didn't mean she couldn't return.

Briony looked around the clearing, committing every detail to memory—the circle of bare trees, the burned post, the exact location where The Channel lay buried in ash. She would come back. Soon. And when she did, she would come prepared. She would bring protective herbs, salt, prayers, whatever was needed to approach this tool safely and use it to communicate with Elsbeth's spirit.

Because now she understood what she had to do. If she wanted to break this curse, if she wanted to save Lila and herself and the village, she needed to speak directly with Elsbeth. She needed to understand what the curse wanted, what would allow Elsbeth's spirit to finally rest.

And The Channel was the only way to do that.

Carefully, reverently, Briony covered the board with ash and leaves once more, hiding it just as she had found it. She didn't know if anyone else ever came to this clearing, but she wanted to make sure the relic would be here when she returned.

"I'll come back," she whispered to the empty air, to the spirit she could feel watching from somewhere beyond sight. "I promise. I'll find a way to help you."

For a moment, the clearing was absolutely still. Then, so faintly she almost thought she'd imagined it, Briony felt a breath of warmer air touch her cheek, like a sigh, like an acknowledgment.

She stood quickly, her heart pounding, and turned to leave. Duska was already at the edge of the clearing, waiting for her, his ears pricked forward and his eyes reflecting the faint light.

Briony walked back through the forest more quickly than she'd come, following the path that seemed to open before her as if the forest was releasing her. The oppressive silence gradually lifted, and by the time she reached the tree line, she could hear the normal sounds of night—crickets chirping, an owl hooting in the distance, the rustle of wind through leaves.

She emerged from Črni Les and stood for a moment at the forest's edge, breathing hard, her mind reeling from what she'd found. Then she turned and hurried back toward her cottage, toward Lila, toward whatever safety she could find in the ordinary world.

When she reached home, she found everything exactly as she'd left it. Lila was still sleeping peacefully in her cradle, her tiny fist curled beneath her chin. The handprints on the wall hadn't moved or changed. The cottage was warm and quiet.

Briony knelt beside the cradle and watched her daughter sleep, her hand reaching out to stroke Lila's soft red hair. The baby stirred slightly at the touch but didn't wake.

"I found it," Briony whispered, her voice barely audible in the quiet room. "I found The Channel. The thing that can help us understand what's happening, what Elsbeth needs. Tomorrow I'll talk to Ana about it. I'll tell her everything I saw, and we'll figure out how to use it safely. We'll gather protective herbs, we'll prepare properly, and then... then we'll use it to communicate with Elsbeth's spirit. We'll find out what she wants, what will allow her to rest. And then we'll break this curse. I promise you, my darling. I promise you with everything I am. I'll do whatever it takes to keep you safe."

She paused, listening to the steady rhythm of Lila's breathing, finding comfort in the simple proof that her daughter was alive and well and here with her.

"You deserve a life without fear," Briony continued softly. "You deserve to grow up in a world where people don't look at you with suspicion just because of who your mother is. You deserve happiness and safety and love. And I'm going to give you that world, even if I have to tear down this curse with my bare hands."

She leaned down and pressed a gentle kiss to Lila's forehead, breathing in that sweet baby scent that always made her feel both fiercely protective and achingly vulnerable.

"No matter what happens," Briony continued, her voice thick with emotion, "I want you to know that you are loved. You are wanted. You are my entire world. And I will fight for you with every breath in my body. The curse won't have you. I won't let it. Do you hear me? I won't let anything in this world or the next take you from me."

Lila made a small sound in her sleep, and one tiny hand opened and closed, as if reaching for something, or someone, in her dreams.

Briony stayed there for a long time, kneeling beside the cradle, watching over her daughter as the night deepened around them. Outside, the wind picked up, rattling the shutters and making the old cottage creak and settle. In the distance, she could hear the howl of wolves in the hills and the faint, ghostly whisper of the forest.

But inside, in this small room lit only by a single candle, there was warmth and safety and love.

And for now, that was enough.

Tomorrow, she would return to the clearing with Ana's guidance. Tomorrow, she would begin the dangerous work of communicating with Elsbeth's spirit. Tomorrow, she would start down the path that would either save them all or destroy her.

But tonight, she would simply be a mother watching over her sleeping child, holding back the darkness for one more night, finding strength in love and determination in the face of impossible odds.

Because that's what mothers do. They stand between their children and the world's dangers. They refuse to yield. They refuse to give up.

And Briony was her mother's daughter, a midwife's daughter, a healer's daughter. She came from a long line of strong women who had faced hardship and persecution and tragedy, and had survived.

She would survive this too. She had to.

For Lila's sake, if not for her own.

The candle burned low as the night wore on, casting flickering shadows across the walls. And through it all, Briony kept her vigil, a silent guardian against the darkness, waiting for the dawn and whatever challenges it might bring.

Chapter 4:

The First Game

Briony hadn't meant to leave the house before dawn, but while the moon was still high, Lila had woken restless—whimpering, twisting, her little fists trembling as though touched by the same lingering dread that haunted Briony's dreams. Also unable to settle, Briony had bundled Lila into a blanket and walked quickly through the quiet village to Ana's.

Ana hadn't asked questions. She had simply opened the door, taken one look at Briony's face, and ushered them in. And so Briony had spent the rest of the night in Ana's small guest room, Lila sleeping beside her in a borrowed cradle.

When dawn finally broke, Briony was already awake, staring at the ceiling and turning Ana's words over in her mind. *To break the curse, you need to uncover the truth. Go to the place where Elsbeth died.*

She knew what she had to do. Though she'd already entered Črni Les once, the idea of going back alone filled her with a deep, primal fear. The Black Wood had always been a place of dark legends, a forest where people disappeared, where the boundary between the living world and the spirit world grew thin.

But Lila's safety depended on her courage.

After a simple breakfast of bread and tea, Briony began her preparations. Ana helped her gather supplies, moving through the house with practiced efficiency.

"You'll need protection," Ana said, pulling down bundles of dried herbs from the rafters. "Sage, for warding off dark spirits. Rosemary, to keep your mind clear and focused. Thyme, for courage." She handed each bundle to Briony, who placed them carefully in her leather satchel.

"Will these be enough?" Briony asked, her voice betraying her nervousness.

"Nothing is ever enough when dealing with the supernatural," Ana replied honestly. "But they will help. And you'll need food and water. There's no telling how long you'll be in the forest. Take this." She handed Briony a small cloth bundle containing bread, cheese, and dried fruit, along with a waterskin.

"And this," Ana added, producing a small notebook and a piece of charcoal. "Write down anything you see or learn. Sometimes the details we think we'll remember are the first to slip away, especially when dealing with spirits."

Briony tucked the notebook into her satchel alongside the herbs and food. "Thank you, Ana. For everything."

Ana placed both hands on Briony's shoulders, looking her directly in the eyes. "Listen to me carefully. When you return to the place where Elsbeth died, you must be respectful. Elsbeth was wronged, terribly wronged, but that doesn't mean her spirit is safe. Pain and anger can twist even the kindest soul. Be cautious. Be humble. And if at any point you feel you're in true danger, leave immediately. Do you understand?"

Briony nodded, swallowing hard. "I understand."

"Good." Ana's expression softened slightly. "Lila will be safe here with Marko and me. Don't worry about her. Focus on what you need to do."

Briony went to the cradle where Lila was sleeping peacefully, her tiny chest rising and falling with each breath. Briony leaned down and pressed a gentle kiss to her daughter's forehead, breathing in that sweet baby scent.

"I'll be back soon," she whispered. "I promise."

Duska appeared at her feet, meowing insistently. The cat had been restless all morning, pacing and watching Briony with those intelligent green eyes.

"You want to come with me, don't you?" Briony said softly.

Duska meowed again, more urgently this time.

"Alright then. Come on."

And so, with her satchel slung over her shoulder and Duska trotting at her heels, Briony set out for Črni Les.

The walk from Ana's house to the edge of the forest took about thirty minutes. The morning was cool and overcast, with gray clouds hanging low in the sky and a damp chill in the air that promised rain before nightfall. As Briony walked, she passed through the village, keeping her head down and avoiding eye contact with anyone she saw.

The village felt different today, heavier somehow, as if the weight of the curse was pressing down on everything. She saw more signs of decay: a garden completely overtaken by black mold, a dead bird lying in the middle of the road, an old woman sitting on her doorstep, weeping quietly.

Briony's resolve strengthened. This had to end. Whatever was happening, whatever darkness had been awakened by the handprints in her cottage, it was affecting everyone. She had to find a way to stop it.

When she finally reached the tree line of Črni Les, Briony paused. The forest loomed before her, dark and forbidding, its ancient trees standing like silent sentinels. The air here was noticeably colder, and there was an odd quality to the silence, as if the forest was holding its breath, waiting.

Briony took a deep breath, squared her shoulders, and stepped into the shadows of the Black Wood.

The change was immediate and unsettling. The moment she crossed the threshold of the forest, the temperature dropped sharply, and the sounds of the outside world, birdsong, the rustle of wind through grass, the distant voices of villagers, all fell away into absolute silence.

Even her footsteps seemed muffled, absorbed by the thick layer of moss and fallen leaves that carpeted the forest floor. Duska stayed close to her legs, his tail low and his ears swiveling nervously.

Briony followed the deer trail north, her eyes scanning the trees around her. The forest was ancient, she could feel it in the gnarled trunks and twisted branches, in the way the roots seemed to reach out across the path like skeletal fingers. Mist clung to the ground in thick patches, swirling around her ankles as she walked.

Time seemed to move strangely here. Briony couldn't tell if she'd been walking for minutes or hours. The gray light filtering through the canopy never changed, remaining constant and dim. There were no landmarks, no signs of human presence, just trees and mist and silence.

Briony retraced her steps from the night before and continued walking. Her heart was pounding now, and her hands felt clammy despite the cold. She could sense something ahead, a heaviness in the air, a wrongness that made her skin prickle with unease.

And then she found it. The clearing. In the dim morning light, Briony could see more than she had last time: A perfect circle of bare trees, their branches reaching toward the sky like supplicating arms. The ground within the circle was covered in a layer of fine gray ash that looked almost like snow. Nothing grew here. No moss, no grass, no flowers. Just ash and bare earth.

In the center of the clearing stood the charred remains of a wooden post, its surface blackened and splintered. This was where Elsbeth had been tied. This was where she had burned.

Briony felt tears sting her eyes. The weight of the tragedy that had occurred here pressed down on her like a physical force. She could almost hear the echoes of Elsbeth's screams, could almost smell the smoke and burning flesh.

"I'm so sorry," Briony whispered to the empty clearing. "What they did to you was wrong. It was evil. You didn't deserve any of it."

For a moment, nothing happened. The clearing remained silent and still. Then Duska let out a low, warning growl.

Briony's gaze dropped to the ground near the burned post, and her breath caught. There, still half-buried in the ash, was The Channel. She knelt down carefully and brushed away the fine gray powder, revealing the rectangular board made of aged, blackened wood.

Briony held her breath as she examined the symbols and letters that covered the board. The symbols in the center circle seemed to pulse with hidden meaning. And resting in the middle of the board was the heart-shaped piece of wood, worn smooth from years of use.

The wooden plank.

Briony reached out tentatively to touch the board, then hesitated. This was a tool for communicating with spirits, with the dead. If she touched it, if she used it, there was no telling what might happen.

But wasn't that why she'd come here? To communicate with Elsbeth's spirit? To find out what the curse wanted, what would allow Elsbeth to rest?

Briony took a deep breath and placed her fingers on the heart-shaped plank.

The reaction was immediate. A shock of cold energy ran up her arm, and the air in the clearing seemed to grow even colder. The mist at the edges of the clearing began to swirl and thicken, moving in slow, deliberate circles.

Briony kept her hand steady on the plank, fighting the urge to pull away. She focused her thoughts, trying to calm the fear that threatened to overwhelm her.

"Elsbeth Korrin," she said aloud, her voice shaking slightly. "My name is Briony. I'm an apprentice midwife, and I've come to speak with you. Handprints appeared in my home, above my daughter's cradle. Please... I need to understand why. I need to know what you want."

For several long moments, nothing happened. The clearing remained silent except for the soft whisper of wind through the bare branches overhead.

Then the plank began to move.

It slid slowly across the board beneath Briony's fingers, moving with purpose and deliberation. She wasn't pushing it, she was certain of that, but it moved nonetheless, gliding from letter to letter.

H-E-L-P

Briony's heart raced. "Help? You need help?"

The plank moved again.

Y-E-S

"What kind of help? What do you need from me?"

The plank circled the board, as if gathering energy, then began spelling out another message, faster this time.

T-R-U-T-H

"The truth?" Briony said. "You want the truth to be known? About what the elders did to you?"

Y-E-S

Briony's mind raced. "But how? How am I supposed to make people believe what happened centuries ago?"

The plank moved to one of the symbols on the board, a flame. Then it moved to another symbol, a book, then to a third, a key.

Briony frowned, trying to interpret the meaning. "Fire... a book... a key. I don't understand."

The plank began moving again, spelling out words.

R-E-C-O-R-D-S

"Records?" Briony said. "There are records of what happened?"

Y-E-S

"Where? Where are they?"

V-I-L-L-A-G-E

"In the village? Where in the village?"

The plank moved decisively.

L-I-B-R-A-R-Y

Briony's breath caught. The village library. Of course. That's where all the old records were kept, birth records, death records, property records. If there was any documentation of what had happened to Elsbeth, it would be there.

"Thank you," Briony whispered. "I'll search for them. I promise."

The plank moved one more time, slowly and with what felt like great effort.

D-A-U-G-H-T-E-R

Briony's blood ran cold. "My daughter? Lila? Is she in danger?"

The plank slid to the symbol for "yes," then moved again.

P-R-O-T-E-C-T

"I am protecting her," Briony said urgently. "She's safe with Ana. What else can I do?"

The plank moved to a new position on the board, indicating a series of symbols Briony hadn't noticed before: a circle, a shield, a branch. Each symbol seemed to glow faintly for a moment, as if illuminated from within, before fading back to normal.

Then it spelled out one final message, moving slowly as if the energy required for communication was draining away:

T-A-L-I-S-M-A-N

"A talisman?" Briony said urgently, sensing the connection was weakening. "I need to make a talisman to protect her?"

Y-E-S

"What kind? What do I need to..."

But the plank stilled beneath her fingers before she could finish the question. Briony sensed that the communication was ending, the fragile bridge between worlds beginning to collapse. The energy in the clearing was beginning to dissipate rapidly, the mist retreating back toward the edges of the circle like water draining from a basin.

The temperature began to rise slightly, though the air remained cold. The oppressive weight that had hung over the clearing lifted gradually, and Briony could hear sounds filtering back in from the surrounding forest, the distant call of a bird, the rustle of leaves, the creak of branches in the wind.

"Wait," Briony said quickly. "Please, I need to know more. What kind of talisman? How do I make it? What do you..."

But it was too late. The connection was broken. The plank lay still and lifeless beneath her hand, just a piece of wood once more.

Briony sat back on her heels, her mind reeling. She'd done it. She'd actually communicated with Elsbeth's spirit. And she'd received answers—or at least, the beginning of answers.

Records in the village library. A talisman for protection. The truth that needed to be uncovered.

She pulled out the notebook Ana had given her and quickly wrote down everything that had happened, every word that had been spelled out, every symbol the plank had indicated. Her hand shook as she wrote, but she forced herself to be thorough. These details might be crucial.

When she was finished, Briony carefully covered The Channel with ash and leaves once more, hiding it as it had been. She didn't know if she would need to return to this clearing, but if she did, she wanted the board to be here, waiting.

"Thank you, Elsbeth," she said softly to the empty air. "I'll do everything I can to help you. I promise."

As she stood to leave, Briony felt something shift in the atmosphere, not threatening, but almost... hopeful. As if her promise had been heard and accepted.

Duska meowed softly and started back toward the path. Briony followed, her mind already turning toward her next steps. She needed to get back to Ana's house, to make sure Lila was safe. And then she needed to figure out how to search the village library without arousing suspicion.

If there were records that proved Elsbeth's innocence, records that documented the elders' crime, then finding them could be the key to breaking the curse.

And if there were instructions for creating a protective talisman, Ana would know how to interpret them. Ana knew the old ways, the old protections. Between the two of them, they could keep Lila safe while Briony worked to uncover the truth.

As Briony walked back through the dim forest, her mind was already racing ahead, planning her next steps. She would need to talk to Ana about the talisman. Ana would know what symbols to use, what materials were needed, what blessings or incantations might activate its protective power. And the library... she would need to find a way to search through the records without drawing attention to herself. The village was already suspicious of her. If they caught her digging through old documents about Elsbeth's death, they might see it as proof that she really was a witch.

But despite the challenges ahead, Briony felt something she hadn't felt since the first handprint appeared in her cottage: hope.

Not the blind, foolish hope of someone who doesn't understand the danger they face. But the determined, clear-eyed hope of someone who finally has a path forward, even if that path is steep and treacherous.

The journey ahead would be dangerous. She would have to search through old records, decipher cryptic clues, and create a protection she didn't fully understand. And all the while, the curse would continue to spread through the village, continuing to mark and threaten and destroy. The handprints might multiply. The supernatural activity might intensify. The villagers' fear and suspicion might turn to outright violence.

But now she had direction. Now she had a purpose. Now she had guidance from the very spirit at the heart of the curse.

And most importantly, now she knew that Elsbeth wasn't just a vengeful spirit bent on mindless destruction. She was a victim seeking justice, a woman who had been murdered and silenced centuries ago and was now calling out across the void of death for someone, anyone, to finally tell the truth about what had been done to her.

Briony could do that. She would do that. She had to.

For Elsbeth, whose name had been dragged through the mud and whose memory had been twisted into a monster story to frighten children. For Lila, who deserved to grow up free from the shadow of this ancient curse. For Ana and all the other midwives who had lived in fear of being the next target. For all the women throughout history who had been blamed, persecuted, and destroyed simply for possessing knowledge and power that others feared.

She would uncover the truth, no matter what it cost her. She would break this curse, or die trying.

Because that's what mothers do. They protect their children, even when it means facing the darkness head-on. Even when it means risking everything.

And Briony was her mother's daughter, a midwife's daughter, a healer's daughter. She had the strength of generations of women flowing through her veins. She would not fail.

She couldn't afford to.

Chapter 5:

Growing Darkness

Briony returned to Ana's house just as the sun was beginning its descent toward the horizon, painting the sky in shades of amber and crimson. Her clothes were damp from the mist of Črni Les, and her boots were caked with mud and ash, but her mind was clear and focused in a way it hadn't been since the handprints first appeared.

Ana met her at the door, relief flooding her face. "Thank the heavens. I was beginning to worry. Come in, quickly, you're shivering."

Inside, the house was warm and bright, lit by candles and the cheerful fire crackling in the hearth. Marko was sitting in a rocking chair with Lila in his arms, humming a soft lullaby. The baby was awake and content, her little hands reaching up toward his weathered face.

"She's been an angel," Marko said with a warm smile. "Ate well, slept well, barely fussed at all."

Briony's heart swelled with gratitude and love. She crossed the room and took Lila from Marko's arms, pressing her face against her daughter's soft hair and breathing in that sweet, innocent scent.

"Thank you," she whispered. "Both of you. I don't know what I'd do without you."

"You'd manage," Ana said practically, but her eyes were kind. "You're stronger than you think, Briony. Now, come sit. Tell us everything that happened."

Over mugs of hot tea and thick slices of bread with honey, Briony recounted her journey into the forest. She told them about finding the clearing, about discovering The Channel buried in the ash. She described the communication with Elsbeth's spirit, the plank moving beneath her fingers, spelling out messages letter by letter.

"She said there are records," Briony explained, pulling out her notebook and showing them the notes she'd made. "In the village library. Documents that might prove what really happened to her. And she said I need to make a talisman to protect Lila."

Ana listened intently, her expression growing more thoughtful as Briony spoke. When Briony finished, Ana was quiet for a long moment, staring into the fire.

"A talisman," she finally said. "Yes, that makes sense. The old protections, they require intention, focus, and a connection to the person you're trying to shield. I can help you with that. We'll need hawthorn wood, which I have. And salt, iron filings, and a few specific herbs. But more importantly, it will need to be blessed by someone with midwife's blood. Someone who carries the same calling as Elsbeth did."

"You," Briony said.

Ana nodded. "I can bless it, give it the power it needs. But the library..." She frowned. "That will be more difficult. The village library is in the old chapel building, and it's only open on certain days. And even then, the elders keep close watch over the oldest records. They won't take kindly to you searching through them."

"I'll have to be careful," Briony said. "But I have to try. If there's proof that Elsbeth was innocent, if there's documentation of what the elders did..."

"It could change everything," Ana finished. "Or it could get you killed."

The words hung heavy in the air.

"I know the risks," Briony said quietly. "But what choice do I have? The curse is spreading. It won't stop until the truth is told."

Ana reached across the table and squeezed her hand. "Then we'll do this together. Tomorrow, you can go into the village to see what people are saying, to get a sense of how bad things have become. And we'll begin work on the talisman. In a few days, when the library is open, you can search for the records. But for tonight, you need to rest. You've been through enough for one day."

Briony wanted to argue, wanted to say that there was no time to rest, that every moment wasted was another moment Lila was in danger. But exhaustion was settling into her bones, and she knew Ana was right. She needed to be strong and clearheaded for what lay ahead.

That night, Briony slept fitfully in Ana's guest room, with Lila safe beside her and Duska curled at the foot of the bed. Her dreams were troubled, filled with burning hands and whispered accusations, with black handprints spreading across walls like ink in water.

The next morning dawned gray and overcast, with heavy clouds hanging low and threatening rain. After a simple breakfast, Briony prepared to make a trip into the village center. She needed supplies—food, lamp oil, a few other necessities—but more than that, she needed to hear what people were saying. She needed to understand how much the curse had spread, how much danger she was really in.

Ana offered to watch Lila again, and Briony gratefully accepted. She wrapped herself in her cloak, pulled the hood up to partially obscure her face, and set out toward the village market with Duska trotting at her heels.

The walk to the market square took about fifteen minutes, and with every step, Briony noticed more signs of the curse's influence. Gardens that had been thriving just days ago were now withered and black, the plants twisted as if they'd been struck by blight. She passed a farmhouse where all the chickens lay dead in their coop, their bodies stiff and their eyes glassy. An old woman sat on her doorstep, rocking back and forth and muttering prayers under her breath.

The village itself felt different, heavier, darker, as if a storm cloud had settled over it and refused to move. The usual sounds of daily life—children laughing, dogs barking, the ring of the blacksmith's hammer—were muted and subdued. People moved through the streets with their heads down and their voices low, casting suspicious glances at their neighbors.

When Briony reached the market square, she found it half-empty. Only a handful of vendors had set up their stalls, and even fewer customers moved among them. The atmosphere was tense, fearful.

Briony kept her hood up and moved quietly from stall to stall, buying a few small items—a loaf of bread, some dried beans, a handful of carrots that looked only slightly wilted. But mostly, she listened.

"My youngest hasn't stopped coughing for three days now," a woman was saying to the baker. "Nothing I give her helps. It's like the sickness has claws in her lungs and won't let go."

"My husband says we should leave," another woman replied. "Pack up and go to my sister's village in the mountains. But where would we get the coin for that? And besides, what if we carry the curse with us?"

"It's that girl," a man's voice said from nearby. Briony froze, recognizing the speaker as Miha, the blacksmith. "The one with the bastard baby. She's the cause of all this. Mark my words."

"How do you figure?" someone else asked.

"My grandfather told me stories," Miha said, his voice low and intense. "About midwives and curses. About women who deal in blood and birth, standing on the threshold between life and death. They say such women can call down darkness if they're not careful. And this girl, Briony, she's not even a real midwife yet. Just an apprentice, and one who got herself with child out of wedlock. That kind of shame brings bad luck."

"I heard the handprints appeared in her cottage first," a woman added. "The black marks, just like in the old stories."

"See?" Miha said triumphantly. "She's marked. The curse started with her. If we want it to end, we need to deal with her."

"What are you suggesting?" the other man asked nervously.

"I'm suggesting we do what our forefathers should have done," Miha said darkly. "Drive her out. Or better yet..."

He didn't finish the sentence, but the implication hung in the air like a noose.

Briony's blood ran cold. She clutched her basket tighter and turned to leave, trying to move quietly and draw no attention to herself.

But Duska chose that moment to meow loudly, and the sound cut through the low murmur of conversation like a knife.

Several heads turned toward Briony. She saw recognition dawn on Miha's face, saw his eyes narrow with suspicion and anger.

"Well, well," he said loudly. "Look who's here. The witch herself."

Briony's heart began to race. She turned and started walking quickly away from the market, but Miha's voice followed her.

"What's the matter, girl? Afraid to face us? Afraid we'll see the truth written on your guilty face?"

Other voices joined in, growing louder and more hostile.

"She's got her demon cat with her!"

"Probably casting spells right now!"

"Someone should stop her!"

Briony broke into a run. She abandoned the market basket, letting it fall to the ground as she fled through the narrow streets with Duska racing ahead of her. Behind her, she could hear footsteps and angry shouts.

"There she goes! After her!"

"Don't let her get away!"

Briony's breath came in ragged gasps as she ran, her cloak tangling around her legs. She took a sharp turn down an alley, then another, trying to lose her pursuers in the maze of back streets that she'd known since childhood.

Finally, she burst out onto a quiet lane and pressed herself against the wall of a building, her heart pounding so hard she thought it might break through her ribs. She could still hear voices in the distance, but they were moving away now, searching in the wrong direction.

Duska pressed against her ankles, his body tense and his tail low.

"It's alright," Briony whispered, though she knew it wasn't. Nothing was alright.

A woman's voice cut through the air, sharp and accusing: "What have you done, witch?"

Briony spun around to find an old woman standing in the doorway of a nearby house, her face twisted with fear and anger. She recognized her, Margareta, one of the village's eldest residents, a woman who had been kind to Briony when she was a child.

But there was no kindness in her eyes now.

"I haven't done anything," Briony said, her voice shaking. "Please, you have to believe me. I'm not responsible for what's happening. I'm trying to help, I'm trying to stop it."

"Liar!" the woman spat. "My grandson is sick. My garden is dead. The curse is your doing, and everyone knows it!"

"No," Briony said desperately. "The curse isn't mine. It's old, older than any of us. It started centuries ago, with Elsbeth Korrin. I'm trying to break it, but I need time. Please..."

But the old woman had already turned away, slamming her door shut.

Briony stood alone in the street, tears streaming down her face. The villagers had turned against her completely. There would be no reasoning with them, no convincing them of her innocence. Fear had poisoned their hearts, just as it had poisoned the hearts of the elders who had murdered Elsbeth all those years ago.

She had to get back to Ana's house. She had to get to Lila.

Briony ran through the streets, taking back ways and avoiding the main roads. By the time she reached Ana's house, she was gasping for breath and her legs were shaking with exhaustion.

Ana opened the door before Briony could even knock, her face pale with worry. "I heard the commotion from here. Come inside, quickly."

Briony stumbled into the house and collapsed into a chair, her whole body trembling. Ana brought her water and wrapped a blanket around her shoulders.

"They think I'm causing the curse," Briony said through her tears, her voice breaking on the words. "They called me a witch. Miha was talking about... about 'dealing' with me. Like they dealt with Elsbeth. They want to drive me out. Or worse. Or..."

She couldn't finish the sentence, but Ana understood. The fear in Briony's eyes said everything that words couldn't.

"I know," Ana said grimly, her own expression troubled. "I feared this would happen. History repeating itself, just as the curse intended. The village is looking for someone to blame for their suffering, and you're an easy target. An outsider, unmarried, with a child and no husband to protect you. And a midwife's apprentice, the same calling as Elsbeth. You fit the pattern perfectly."

"But I haven't done anything!" Briony protested desperately. "I'm trying to help! I'm trying to break the curse, not spread it!"

"I believe you," Ana said, reaching out to take Briony's shaking hands. "But belief and truth don't matter when people are afraid. Fear makes monsters of ordinary folk. It makes them do terrible things in the name of protection."

"What am I going to do?" Briony asked, fresh tears spilling down her cheeks. "I can't stay in the village, they'll kill me. But I can't leave, not until I break the curse. And I can't bring Lila anywhere near the village center. It's not safe for her. But it's not safe anywhere!"

Ana was quiet for a moment, thinking. Then she spoke, her voice firm and decisive. "You'll stay here, with us. Marko and I will keep you and Lila safe. And tonight, when the village is sleeping, we'll make the talisman. Then, when the time is right, you'll go to the library and search for the records. It's the only way."

"But what if they come here?" Briony asked. "What if they find us?"

"Then we'll face them together," Ana said. "I've lived in this village my whole life, and I've earned their respect. They may fear you, but they won't harm you while you're under my protection. At least, not yet."

It wasn't much reassurance, but it was all they had.

That evening, after Lila had been fed and put to sleep, Ana and Briony set to work on the talisman. They worked by candlelight at the kitchen table, with Marko keeping watch at the window in case any villagers approached.

Ana had gathered all the necessary materials: a small piece of hawthorn wood, carved into a smooth disc about the size of a coin; iron filings, collected from Marko's workshop; salt, blessed by the village priest years ago; and dried herbs—sage for protection, rowan for warding off evil, vervain for strength.

"The talisman works through intention," Ana explained as she worked. "Every material we use carries symbolic meaning. The hawthorn represents protection and the threshold between worlds. The iron repels malevolent spirits. The salt creates barriers. The herbs lend their specific properties."

She carved a simple symbol into the hawthorn disc, a circle with a cross through its center, the ancient sign of protection. Then she pressed the iron filings into the wood, mixing them with a paste made from the herbs and a few drops of her own blood.

"Midwife's blood," Ana said quietly. "To connect the talisman to Elsbeth's calling, to show respect for what she was."

When the talisman was complete, Ana held it in both hands and closed her eyes. She spoke in a low voice, words in a language Briony didn't recognize, perhaps the old tongue that midwives had used for centuries to bless and protect.

The talisman began to glow faintly, a soft golden light that pulsed like a heartbeat. Then the glow faded, and Ana opened her eyes.

"It is done," she said, handing the talisman to Briony. "Keep this with Lila at all times. It won't stop the curse entirely, but it will shield her from the worst of its effects. As long as she wears this, the handprints cannot claim her."

Briony took the talisman with trembling hands. It was warm to the touch, and she could feel a faint vibration running through it, the echo of Ana's blessing, the power of generations of midwives flowing through this small piece of wood.

"Thank you," Briony whispered. "Thank you so much."

She went immediately to the room where Lila slept and carefully threaded a leather cord through the hole in the talisman. Then she placed it around her daughter's neck, tucking it beneath the baby's gown where it would rest close to her heart.

Lila stirred briefly but didn't wake, her tiny chest rising and falling with steady, peaceful breaths.

Briony stood over the cradle for a long time, watching her daughter sleep, feeling the weight of what lay ahead pressing down on her shoulders like a physical burden she could barely carry. The candlelight flickered across Lila's peaceful face, and Briony marveled at how innocent she looked, how untouched by the darkness swirling around them.

The village had turned against her. The curse was spreading like poison through every street, every home, every heart. People were suffering, dying, their lives being destroyed by forces they didn't understand. And they all blamed her. They saw her as the source of their pain, when in reality, she was just as much a victim as they were, maybe more so.

But now Lila was protected. The talisman would shield her from the worst of the curse's effects. Now Briony had a weapon blessed by a midwife's hand and a midwife's blood, carrying the power of generations. And soon, very soon, she would go to the library and search for the records that would prove Elsbeth's innocence. She would find the truth that had been buried for centuries, and she would drag it into the light no matter who tried to stop her.

She would break this curse, no matter what it cost her. No matter how much danger she had to face, how much pain she had to endure, how many risks she had to take.

Even if it meant facing the darkness alone. Even if it meant sacrificing everything.

Because that's what mothers did. They protected their children, no matter the cost.

And Briony would protect Lila, or die trying.

As she finally turned away from the cradle and prepared to get some rest herself, Briony whispered one more promise into the quiet room, a promise to herself, to Lila, to Elsbeth's restless spirit, and to all the midwives who had come before.

"This ends with me. I won't let it continue. I won't let another generation suffer for sins they didn't commit. The truth will come out, and the curse will be broken. I swear it."

And with those words still hanging in the air like a vow, Briony finally allowed herself to sleep, knowing that tomorrow would bring new challenges, new dangers, and perhaps, if she was lucky and brave and strong enough, new hope.

Chapter 6:

Uncovering the Curse

Briony woke before dawn to the sound of rain pattering against the windows of Ana's house. She'd barely slept, her mind too full of fear and determination to allow for true rest. Every time she'd closed her eyes, she'd seen the faces of the angry villagers, heard Miha's dark threats, felt the weight of their hatred pressing down on her.

But Lila had slept peacefully through the night, the talisman resting against her chest, glowing faintly whenever Briony checked on her. That small comfort gave Briony the strength to face what lay ahead.

She rose quietly, careful not to wake her daughter, and made her way to the kitchen. She found Ana already there, sitting at the table with a large, leather-bound book spread open before her. The book was old, its pages yellowed and brittle, its cover cracked with age.

"Is that—?" Briony began.

"The village record book I took from the library," Ana said quietly. "Years ago, when I first learned the truth about Elsbeth, I borrowed it to study what had happened. I never returned it. I thought... I thought if I kept it hidden, I might prevent the curse from taking hold again." She looked up at Briony, her eyes red-rimmed from lack of sleep. "I was wrong."

Briony sat down across from her, her heart beginning to race. "What have you found?"

Ana turned the book so Briony could see. The page was covered in cramped, faded handwriting, entries from centuries past, chronicling births and deaths, marriages and departures.

"Here," Ana said, pointing to an entry dated nearly three hundred years ago. "This is Elsbeth's last official mention in the village records."

Briony leaned closer and read the entry aloud: "The widow Elsbeth Korrin, midwife, has departed Senčna Vas. May God guide her path."

"That's all?" Briony said, disappointment flooding through her. "They just said she left?"

"That was the official story," Ana confirmed. "The lie the elders told to cover up what they'd really done. But look at the entries that come after."

Ana flipped through several pages, showing Briony entry after entry that told a different story. Within months of Elsbeth's "departure," the village had been struck by disaster. Crops failed. Livestock died. A fever swept through the children, taking three lives in one week. Strange accidents occurred—a barn collapsing without cause, a well suddenly running dry, a fire consuming half the village center on a night with no lightning and no careless flames.

And through it all, there were the handprints. Black marks appearing on walls, doors, cradles. Always near the homes of midwives.

"It's all documented," Ana said quietly. "Every generation, the curse returns. And every time, it targets a midwife, usually one with a young child. Some of them fled. Some of them died. Some simply... disappeared."

Briony felt sick. "How many?"

"At least a dozen, over the centuries," Ana said. "Probably more. Not all of them would have been recorded." She turned to another page. "But there's something else. Look at this entry, from about fifty years after Elsbeth's death."

Briony read the entry Ana indicated:

> *The midwife Katarina, accused of consorting with dark spirits, has confessed to her crimes and been banished from the village. Her infant daughter, afflicted with the mark, was taken to the sisters at the convent for purification. May the Lord have mercy on their souls.*

"The mark," Briony breathed. "The handprints."

"Yes," Ana said. "The curse demands a midwife and her child. That's the pattern. Every time the handprints appear, they target a woman in our calling and her baby. And every time, the village responds with fear and violence, repeating the same sin that created the curse in the first place."

Briony's hands clenched into fists on the table. "They keep making the same mistake. They keep blaming the midwives instead of acknowledging what was done to Elsbeth."

"That's how curses work," Ana said sadly. "They feed on repeated patterns, on unlearned lessons. As long as the truth remains hidden, as long as the injustice is never acknowledged, the curse will continue."

"Then we have to break the pattern," Briony said firmly. "We have to find proof, real proof, of what the elders did. Something that can't be denied or explained away."

Ana was quiet for a moment, then she spoke slowly, choosing her words carefully. "There may be such proof.

I've heard whispers, over the years, of a confession. One of the elders who participated in Elsbeth's execution supposedly wrote down what they'd done, overcome by guilt. His wife hid the document, afraid of what would happen if it was discovered."

Briony's heart leaped. "Where? Where is it?"

"If the stories are true, it's hidden in the old chapel," Ana said. "Somewhere in the building where the village keeps its most sacred and secret things. But I don't know exactly where, and I've never had the courage to search for it myself."

"I'll search for it," Briony said immediately. "I'll find it."

"The chapel is only open for services on holy days," Ana warned. "And even then, you'd be watched. The elders guard their secrets well."

"Then I'll go when it's closed," Briony said. "At night, when no one's watching."

"That's breaking and entering," Ana said. "If you're caught."

"I'm already being hunted," Briony interrupted. "What's one more crime to add to the list? Besides, if this confession exists, if it proves what happened to Elsbeth, it could change everything. The villagers would have to face the truth."

Ana looked at her for a long moment, then slowly nodded. "You're right. It's a risk we have to take." She reached across the table and took Briony's hand. "But not tonight. You're exhausted, and you need to be sharp for this. Rest today. Spend time with Lila. Let me make some inquiries about the chapel, find out if there are any stories about where documents might be hidden. Then tomorrow night, when you're rested and prepared, we'll make our move."

Briony wanted to argue, but she knew Ana was right. She was running on fear and determination, but those would only carry her so far. She needed to be smart about this.

"Alright," she agreed. "Tomorrow night."

Briony spent the rest of that day in Ana's house, playing with Lila and trying to calm the anxiety that churned in her stomach. Every sound from outside made her jump, convinced that the villagers had come for her. But the day passed quietly, with only the rain and wind for company.

That evening, after Lila had been fed and settled for the night, Ana returned from a carefully casual visit to several of her oldest friends in the village, women who remembered the old stories, who might know something about the chapel's secrets.

"I think I know where the confession might be hidden," Ana said as she hung her damp cloak by the fire. "Old Berta, who tends the chapel, mentioned once that there's a loose stone beneath the altar. Third row from the front, fourth stone from the left. Her grandfather used to be a deacon, and he told her it was a place where the elders hid things they didn't want found."

"Tomorrow night," Briony said. "I'll go tomorrow night."

Ana nodded, then pulled something from her pocket: a large iron key, old and rust-spotted. "This is the key to the chapel's side door. I... borrowed it from Berta's key ring while she was distracted. She'll think she simply misplaced it."

Briony took the key, feeling its weight in her palm. This was really happening. Tomorrow night, she would break into the chapel and search for the confession that could prove Elsbeth's innocence.

The next day passed in a blur of nervous energy and forced calm. Briony went through the motions of caring for Lila, but her mind was elsewhere, planning and preparing for the night ahead.

As evening approached, Marko pulled Briony aside.

"I know what you're planning," he said quietly. "And I want to help. I'll keep watch while you search. If anyone approaches, I'll signal you."

"Marko, you don't have to..."

"Yes, I do," he interrupted gently. "Ana is my wife, and you're like a daughter to us. Whatever danger you're in, we're in it together."

Briony felt tears prick her eyes. "Thank you," she whispered.

When full darkness fell and the village had settled into sleep, Briony and Marko set out. They moved through the streets like shadows, keeping to the darkest corners and avoiding the few lit windows. The rain had stopped, but the night was cold and damp, with clouds obscuring the moon and stars.

The chapel stood at the edge of the village square, a solid stone building with narrow windows and a bell tower that loomed against the dark sky. It looked ancient and imposing, a place of secrets and power.

Marko positioned himself in the shadows near the main road, where he could see anyone approaching. Briony made her way to the side door, her hands shaking as she fit the key into the lock.

The lock turned with a soft click, and the door swung inward.

Briony stepped inside, pulling the door closed behind her. The chapel was pitch black, so she lit the small lantern she'd brought, keeping the light low. The flame cast flickering shadows across the stone walls and the rows of wooden pews.

She moved quickly toward the altar at the front of the chapel. It was a simple stone structure, raised on a platform with three steps. Briony knelt at the base of the altar and began examining the stones.

Third row from the front, fourth stone from the left.

She found the stone Ana had described, slightly smaller than the others, with a crack running along one edge. Briony worked her fingers into the crack and pulled. At first, nothing happened. Then, with a grinding sound, the stone shifted.

She pulled it free, revealing a dark hollow beneath.

Briony held her lantern closer and peered into the space. There, wrapped in oilcloth and covered in dust, was a bundle of papers.

Her heart pounding, Briony reached in and carefully pulled out the bundle. She unwrapped the oilcloth with trembling fingers.

Inside were several sheets of parchment, yellowed with age and covered in faded ink. The handwriting was shaky and uneven, as if written by someone in great distress.

Briony held the first page close to the lantern and began to read.

> *I, Tomás, elder of Senčna Vas, do confess my sins before God and man. What we did to Elsbeth Korrin was murder, pure*

and simple. She was innocent of the charges brought against her. We knew this. We knew, and we burned her anyway.

My daughter died in childbirth, and in my grief, I sought someone to blame. Elsbeth had attended the birth. She did everything she could to save my daughter, but the bleeding would not stop. It was not Elsbeth's fault. It was no one's fault. But I could not accept that.

I convinced the other elders that Elsbeth had brought a curse upon us, that she had used dark magic to harm the village. It was a lie. All of it was a lie. But once the accusation was made, fear spread like wildfire. The villagers demanded action, and we gave it to them.

We took Elsbeth to Črni Les in the dead of night and burned her alive. Her screams will haunt me until the day I die. And as she burned, she cursed us. She said her hands would mark the village, that midwives and their children would suffer as she had suffered, that the truth would come out in blood and fire.

I have tried to forget. I have tried to live as if this sin does not stain my soul. But I cannot. The handprints have begun to appear, just as she promised. Children are falling ill. The crops are failing. Her curse is real.

I write this confession in the hope that someday, someone will find it and tell the truth. Elsbeth Korrin was innocent. We murdered her. We are the criminals, not she. May God forgive us, for I do not think she ever will.

The confession was signed and dated nearly three hundred years ago.

Briony sat back on her heels, clutching the papers to her chest as tears streamed down her face. This was it. This was the proof she had been searching for. A written confession from one of the elders themselves. Not hearsay, not rumor, but a direct admission of guilt, written in the murderer's own hand. Admitting to the false accusation. Admitting to the execution. Admitting that Elsbeth Korrin had been innocent all along.

The weight of what she held in her hands was almost overwhelming. This wasn't just a piece of old parchment. This was justice, delayed by centuries but finally within reach. This was the truth that had been buried and hidden and denied for generations. This was the key to breaking the curse.

With this confession, she could prove Elsbeth's innocence to the entire village. She could force them to confront what their ancestors had done. She could show them that the real evil wasn't Elsbeth's supposed witchcraft, it was the murder committed by frightened men who chose lies over truth, violence over justice.

And if the villagers acknowledged the truth, if they admitted the injustice that had been done... then perhaps Elsbeth's spirit could finally rest. Perhaps the curse that had haunted midwives for centuries could finally be broken.

Briony carefully rewrapped the papers in the oilcloth, handling them as gently as if they were made of glass. She tucked the bundle inside her cloak, pressing it close to her heart where it would be safe and secure.

But as she carefully rewrapped the papers and tucked them inside her cloak, a sound from outside made her freeze.

Voices. Approaching the chapel.

Briony extinguished her lantern and moved quickly toward the side door, her heart racing. She slipped outside just as the voices grew louder and pressed herself against the wall in the shadows.

Through the darkness, she could see a group of men approaching the chapel, Miha among them, carrying torches.

"I tell you, I saw someone go in," one of them was saying. "A figure slipping through the side door."

"The witch," Miha said grimly. "She's inside. We've got her now."

Briony's blood ran cold. She looked around desperately for Marko and saw him in the shadows across the square, gesturing frantically for her to run.

She ran.

She fled through the narrow streets with the sounds of pursuit close behind her, the precious confession pressed against her chest beneath her cloak. The night air was cold against her face, and her breath came in ragged gasps that burned in her lungs. Behind her, she could hear angry shouts and the pounding of boots on wet cobblestones, growing louder as the mob closed the distance.

"There! I see her!"

"Don't let her escape!"

"The witch has something. She was in the chapel!"

Briony's legs pumped harder, her heart racing with fear and determination in equal measure. She had to get back to Ana's house. She had to get to safety. But more importantly, she had to protect the confession. If they caught her, if they took it from her, all of this would be for nothing.

She ducked down a narrow alley, her boots splashing through puddles. Duska appeared from nowhere, racing alongside her with his tail streaming behind him like a dark banner. The cat's presence gave her a strange comfort—she wasn't entirely alone in this desperate flight.

Briony burst out onto a different street and risked a glance over her shoulder. The mob was still there, torches blazing in the darkness, but she'd gained a little distance. She knew these streets better than most of them did. She'd grown up here, played in these alleys as a child, and knew every shortcut and hiding place.

She took another turn, then another, weaving through the maze of the village until she finally saw Ana's house ahead, its windows glowing with welcoming candlelight.

Briony pounded on the door, and it opened immediately. Ana pulled her inside and slammed it shut, throwing the bolt.

"Did you find it?" Ana asked urgently.

Briony pulled the oilcloth bundle from her cloak, her hands shaking with exhaustion and adrenaline. "I found it. The confession. Tomás wrote everything, the false accusation, the murder, all of it. It's all here."

Ana took the bundle reverently, unwrapping it just enough to see the first few lines of the confession. Her eyes widened, and she looked up at Briony with something like awe.

"This changes everything," she breathed.

"I know," Briony said, sinking into a chair as her legs finally gave out. "But the mob is right behind me. They know I took something from the chapel. They're coming."

As if in answer, angry voices rose from the street outside, growing louder as the mob approached.

Marko hurriedly entered through the back door, breathless, his face grim. "Bar the door. Put out most of the candles. We need to make it look like no one's home."

They worked quickly, securing the house and reducing the light to a single candle in the back room where Lila slept, still peaceful and protected by her talisman.

Briony sat in the darkness, clutching the confession to her chest, listening to the sounds of the mob searching the streets outside. They had the truth now. They had the proof.

But tomorrow... tomorrow, they would have to figure out how to make the village listen. How to break through centuries of lies and force them to face what had been done.

Tomorrow, the village would finally know what their ancestors had done. Tomorrow, the truth would come to light.

Tomorrow, the curse would be broken.

She just had to survive the night.

And as she sat there in the darkness, with Ana and Marko standing guard and Lila sleeping peacefully nearby, Briony allowed herself to feel something she hadn't felt in days: hope.

Real, solid, tangible hope.

Because now she had the weapon she needed to end this. Now she had justice in her hands, written in ink and signed with a guilty conscience.

Now, finally, she could save them all.

Chapter 7:

The Curse Tightens

Briony woke to the sound of her own heartbeat pounding in her ears. She must have drifted off to sleep not long after returning home just before dawn, too shaken to stay any longer at Ana and Marko's and too proud to be a burden to them. The gray light seeped through her bedroom curtains, washing the room in cold silver and stretching long shadows across the wooden floorboards.

For a moment, she lay still, trying to convince herself that the previous night had been nothing more than exhaustion playing tricks on her mind—the handprints, the whispers, the breath of cold wind that crept across her skin even though every window and door had been locked tight. She wanted to believe none of it had followed her here.

Then she heard Lila whimper softly from her cradle, and Briony's eyes snapped open.

She sat up slowly, her body aching with a bone-deep exhaustion that sleep had done nothing to cure. The air in the room felt thick and heavy, pressing down on her chest like a physical weight. She could smell something acrid and burnt, though no fire had been lit in the hearth since the night before.

Briony forced herself to stand, her bare feet touching the cold wooden floor. She took three steps toward the cradle before she saw them.

The handprints.

They covered the wall around Lila's cradle now, no longer scattered or isolated. They formed a perfect circle, each soot-black mark overlapping the next, creating an unbroken ring that surrounded her baby like a noose tightening around a neck. The marks seemed to pulse with a dark energy, and as Briony stared at them, she could swear she saw them moving, shifting, spreading, reaching.

"No," she whispered, her voice cracking. "No, no, no."

She rushed to the cradle and scooped Lila into her arms, holding her daughter's warm body against her chest. Lila's eyes fluttered open, and she let out a soft cry that cut through Briony like a blade. The baby was safe, unharmed, but the handprints were so close now. Too close.

Duska appeared at Briony's feet, his dark gray fur standing on end. The cat's green eyes were fixed on the wall, his tail twitching with agitation. A low growl rumbled from his throat, a sound Briony had never heard him make before.

"I see them too," Briony murmured, stroking Lila's soft red hair. Her own hands were trembling. "I see them too."

She backed away from the cradle, unable to tear her gaze from the circle of handprints. In the dim morning light, they looked like the marks of something desperate and angry, something that had been reaching for her daughter all night while Briony slept, helpless and unaware.

The weight of her failure pressed down on her shoulders. She was supposed to protect Lila. That was her only job, her only purpose, and she was failing.

A sudden sound from the front of the cottage made Briony freeze. A sharp crack, like wood splitting. Then another. She clutched Lila tighter and moved toward the doorway of the bedroom, her heart racing.

"Who's there?" she called out, her voice stronger than she felt.

Silence answered her.

Then came the crash.

The sound of shattering glass exploded through the cottage, and Lila began to wail. Briony ran toward the living room, her bare feet slapping against the floor. She stopped in the doorway and stared at the scene before her.

The window overlooking the front path was broken, jagged shards of glass littering the floor like scattered teeth. Cold morning air rushed through the opening, carrying with it the scent of damp earth and pine. And there, in the center of the floor, lay a large rock.

Briony's breath caught in her throat. She approached slowly, careful to avoid the glass, and bent down to examine the rock more closely. Her stomach twisted.

Scrawled across its surface in thick black charcoal was a single word: **WITCH**.

The letters were crude and angry, pressed into the stone with such force that the charcoal had crumbled at the edges. Whoever had thrown this wanted to make sure she understood. They wanted her to know that she was not safe, that they were watching, that they blamed her.

Briony's hands began to shake. She dropped the rock and stepped back, her mind reeling. Lila's cries grew louder, more desperate, and Briony felt her own panic rising to match her daughter's.

"It's alright, sweetheart," she whispered, bouncing Lila gently. "It's alright. We're alright."

But they weren't alright. They weren't safe here anymore.

Briony moved to the broken window and peered outside, her eyes scanning the misty morning landscape. The path leading to her cottage was empty, but she could feel eyes watching her from somewhere in the shadows. The forest pressed close on all sides, its dark trees looming like silent sentinels. Somewhere out there, someone had thrown that rock. Someone who believed she was responsible for the curse, for the handprints, for everything that had gone wrong in Senčna Vas.

And they were not alone in that belief. She had seen it in the faces of the villagers when she walked through town—the fear, the suspicion, the barely concealed hatred. It was only a matter of time before fear turned to action, before suspicion became violence.

Briony turned away from the window and hurried back to her bedroom. She needed to leave. Now. She couldn't stay here with Lila, not with the handprints closing in and the villagers turning against her. There was only one place she could go, only one person she could trust.

Ana.

She moved quickly, gathering Lila's belongings with trembling hands, clean clothes, a soft blanket, the small wooden rattle that Marko had carved for her. She wrapped Lila in a warm shawl and tucked her into the crook of her arm, then grabbed her own cloak from the hook by the door.

Duska wound himself around her ankles, meowing insistently.

"Come on, then," Briony said, her voice thick with unshed tears. "We're going together."

She stepped out into the cold morning air, pulling the door shut behind her. The forest around her cottage seemed darker than usual, the shadows deeper and more oppressive. The mist clung to the ground like ghostly fingers, and the usual sounds of birdsong were absent. Everything felt wrong, as if the world itself was holding its breath.

Briony walked quickly along the narrow path that led from her cottage toward the village, Lila clutched tightly against her chest, Duska trotting at her heels. Every rustle of leaves, every snap of a twig, made her jump. She kept her eyes fixed on the path ahead, trying to ignore the sensation of being watched.

As she approached the outskirts of Senčna Vas, she began to notice the signs of the curse's spread everywhere she looked. A garden that had been lush and green just days before was now withered and brown, the plants blackened and twisted as if struck by a sudden frost. The vegetables that should have been ripening on their vines now hung limp and rotted, coated in a strange gray mold Briony had never seen before.

A thin stray dog lay collapsed near the roadside, its ribs showing through its matted fur, its eyes clouded to a dull white. Briony slowed as she passed, her throat tightening. It wasn't the first dead creature she had encountered. More bodies had appeared along the path, each one another grim warning of how far the curse had spread.

The curse was spreading faster now, its influence seeping into every corner of the village like poison in water. She could feel it in the air itself, a heaviness, a thickness that made each breath feel labored. The mist that clung to the ground seemed darker than usual, almost gray, and it carried with it a faint smell of decay that made her stomach turn.

She heard voices ahead and instinctively pressed herself against the side of a building, her back flat against the rough timber wall, trying to remain unseen. Her heart hammered in her chest as she peered around the corner. Two men stood in the town square, their voices low but urgent, their faces drawn and haggard in the gray morning light.

"Found three more sheep dead this morning," one of them was saying. It was the shepherd named Jozef, a man Briony had known since childhood. His voice was thick with exhaustion and fear. "Throats torn out, but no blood on the ground. No tracks either. It's not natural. No wolf or bear would kill like that."

"Nothing's been natural since the handprints started appearing," the other replied. This was Miha, the blacksmith, a burly man with a thick beard and arms like tree trunks. "My wife says it's the curse. Says we should never have let that girl stay in the village after what happened. Says she's brought the darkness down on us."

"You mean Briony? The midwife's apprentice?"

"Aye. Her and that demon cat of hers. Black as sin, it is. My wife saw it walking past our house two nights ago, and the next morning, our milk had gone sour, and the baby wouldn't stop crying. Mark my words, she's brought this on us. Her and her bastard child. It's witchcraft, plain as day."

Jozef shifted uncomfortably. "I don't know, Miha. Briony's never done anything to hurt anyone. She's helped deliver half the children in this village. Her and Ana both."

"Aye, and maybe that's how she's been cursing us all along," Miha shot back, his voice rising. "Maybe she's been working her dark magic on our children from the moment they drew breath. We should have driven her out when she turned up pregnant with no husband. A woman like that brings shame and trouble."

Briony's chest tightened with anger and fear. She wanted to step out from her hiding place and confront them, to tell them she had done nothing wrong, that she was as much a victim of this curse as they were. But she knew it would do no good. Their fear had already poisoned their hearts against her.

She waited until the men moved on, then hurried past the square and toward Ana's house on the far side of the village. The streets were nearly empty, most of the villagers still inside their homes, but she could feel their eyes on her through the windows. She kept her head down and walked faster.

When she finally reached Ana's door, she knocked urgently, her knuckles rapping against the wood in a desperate rhythm. A moment later, the door swung open, and Ana's worried face appeared.

"Briony?" Ana's eyes widened as she took in the sight of her young apprentice—her pale, frightened face, the baby clutched in her arms, the dark-furred cat at her feet. "What's happened? Come in, quickly."

Briony stumbled inside, and Ana shut the door firmly behind her. Marko appeared from the kitchen, his expression concerned.

"Is it the curse?" he asked quietly.

Briony nodded, unable to speak. Her throat felt tight, and tears burned at the corners of her eyes. Ana gently took Lila from her arms and passed the baby to Marko, who cradled her with practiced ease.

"Sit," Ana said, guiding Briony to a chair by the fire. "Tell me everything."

Briony sank into the chair, her body trembling. The warmth of the fire did nothing to chase away the cold that had settled deep in her bones. She took a shaky breath and began to speak.

She told them about waking to find the handprints forming a complete circle around Lila's cradle, about the rock thrown through her window with the word "witch" scrawled across it in charcoal. She told them about the dead animals she had seen on her way through the village, about the conversation she had overheard in the square.

"They think I'm responsible," she said, her voice breaking. "They think I brought the curse on them. And I don't know how to prove them wrong. I don't know how to stop this."

After a few moments, Briony reached into the folds of her cloak and brought out the aged parchment of Tomás's confession, spreading it out carefully on Ana's kitchen table, her hands still trembling slightly. The confession lay before them, its ink faded but legible, the condemning words written three centuries ago.

"This is it," Briony said, her voice hoarse. "Proof that Elsbeth was innocent. Proof that the elders murdered her."

Ana studied the document, her finger tracing the shaky handwriting. Marko leaned over her shoulder, his face grave.

"It's genuine," Ana said quietly. "The seal, the signature, the style of writing... This is real."

"Then we have what we need!" Briony said, a desperate hope rising in her chest. "We can show this to the village. We can prove she was wrongly killed. Surely that will break the curse?"

But Ana's expression remained troubled. She looked up at Briony, and there was sorrow in her eyes.

"But will they believe it?" she asked gently. "A three-hundred-year-old confession found by the very woman the villagers already suspect? They'll say you forged it. That you created it to protect yourself."

Briony's hope crumbled. "But—"

"And even if they did believe it," Marko added, his voice heavy, "would it be enough? The confession tells us what happened, but curses don't break just because the truth is revealed. Elsbeth's spirit has been bound to this village for centuries. Her pain, her rage—it's deeper than words on paper."

Ana placed her hand over Briony's. "The letter is important. It validates what we suspected, and it may be part of what's needed. But I don't think it's enough by itself. The curse feeds on injustice, yes, but it also feeds on Elsbeth's unresolved spirit. We need to understand what she truly wants, what will allow her to finally rest."

Briony stared at the confession, feeling the weight of those old words. "Then what good is it? What good is proof if it can't save Lila?"

"It's a weapon," Marko said firmly. "Maybe not the only one you need, but a weapon nonetheless. The truth matters, even if the village won't accept it yet. Keep it safe. When the time comes to confront Elsbeth's spirit, to truly break this curse, you'll need every piece of truth there is."

Briony carefully folded the parchment and tucked it into her dress. The confession was real, the proof was real, but the curse was still active. The handprints still multiplied on her walls. The village still suffered.

Proof wasn't enough. She would need something more.

"Then I have to go back to The Channel," Briony said. "I have to speak with Elsbeth directly. I have to find out what she needs—not just acknowledgment of the truth, but justice. Real justice."

Briony's stomach twisted with fear. The memory of her last encounter with The Channel was still vivid in her mind—the cold whispers, the moving plank, the cards that seemed to burn with dark fire. The thought of returning to that clearing, of facing Elsbeth's spirit again, filled her with dread.

But what choice did she have?

"I'll watch Lila," Ana said, as if reading her thoughts. "She'll be safe here with us. Marko and I will guard her with our lives. You focus on breaking this curse."

Briony looked over at Marko, who was rocking Lila gently in his arms. The baby had stopped crying and was staring up at him with wide, curious eyes. Despite everything, the sight brought a small measure of comfort to Briony's aching heart.

"Thank you," she whispered.

Ana squeezed her hands one more time, then released them. "Go. Do what you must. And be careful. Elsbeth's spirit is powerful, and her anger runs deep. Don't underestimate her."

Briony nodded and stood, her legs unsteady beneath her. She walked over to Marko and pressed a gentle kiss to Lila's forehead, breathing in the sweet scent of her daughter's hair.

"I'll come back for you," she promised. "I'll fix this."

Then she turned and walked toward the door, Duska following at her heels. As she stepped back out into the cold morning air, she felt the weight of her decision settle over her like a cloak. There was no turning back now. She had to face The Channel again, had to confront Elsbeth's spirit and find a way to break the curse.

Even if it meant risking everything.

The walk back through the village felt longer than before. The mist had grown thicker, swirling around her ankles and obscuring the path ahead. She kept her head down, avoiding eye contact with anyone she passed. The whispers followed her, soft, insidious, filled with suspicion and fear.

"...saw her leaving Ana's house..."

"...probably cursed her too..."

"...shouldn't be allowed to walk freely..."

Briony clenched her fists and kept walking. Let them whisper. Let them hate her. It didn't matter. All that mattered was Lila and protecting her from the darkness that threatened to swallow them both.

By the time she reached the edge of Črni Les, the sun had climbed higher in the sky, though its light did little to penetrate the thick canopy of trees. The forest loomed before her like a living thing, dark and foreboding. Duska hesitated at the tree line, his ears flattened against his head.

"I know," Briony said softly, reaching down to stroke his fur. "But we have to go in. There's no other way."

She took a deep breath and stepped into the shadows of the Black Wood. The air inside the forest was colder than in the village, and the silence was absolute. No birds sang, no insects buzzed. It was as if the forest itself was waiting, watching.

Briony walked the familiar path toward the clearing, her footsteps muffled by the thick layer of moss and fallen leaves. The trees pressed close on either side, their gnarled branches reaching out like skeletal fingers. She could feel the weight of the forest's attention on her, heavy and oppressive.

When she finally reached the clearing, she stopped at its edge and stared. The space looked exactly as she had left it, the circle of bare trees standing like silent witnesses, the soft carpet of moss covering the ground, the hidden shape of The Channel beneath its covering of leaves and twigs. But there was something different about it now, something darker and more foreboding.

The air felt charged, electric, as if a storm was about to break. The usual sounds of the forest—the rustle of leaves, the distant call of birds, the scurrying of small creatures— were completely absent. It was as if every living thing had fled from this place, sensing the danger that dwelt here.

Briony felt Duska press against her leg, his body tense and wary. The cat's ears were flattened against his head, and his tail was puffed out to twice its normal size. He didn't want to enter the clearing, and Briony couldn't blame him.

But she had no choice.

"Stay close to me," she murmured to Duska, then stepped into the clearing with deliberate, measured steps.

The moment her foot crossed the invisible boundary, the temperature dropped sharply. Her breath misted in the air, and goosebumps rose on her arms beneath her cloak. The mist that had been swirling at the edges of the forest began to creep into the clearing, tendrils of gray vapor winding around the base of the trees like ghostly serpents.

Briony knelt before The Channel in the clearing, the confession letter folded against her heart beneath her dress. She had proof of the elders' crime, written in their own hand. She had the truth about what happened that terrible night.

But she also knew, with a certainty that made her bones ache, that the truth alone wasn't enough.

"I know you were innocent," Briony whispered to the darkness. "I have the confession. I know what they did to you. But you knew that already, didn't you? You've always known."

The air grew colder. The handprints on the trees seemed to pulse with dark energy.

"It's not about me knowing," Briony continued. "It's about what was hidden, what's still hidden. The elder's confession tells me you were murdered, but it doesn't tell me why. It doesn't tell me who truly betrayed you."

She placed her hands on The Channel, feeling the old wood thrumming with spiritual energy.

"Show me, Elsbeth. Show me the whole truth. Not just what the elders did—but who set it in motion. Because I don't think they acted alone. Someone gave them a reason. Someone wanted you dead."

The candles flickered violently. And Elsbeth answered.

The plank began to move.

The game was about to begin again.

Chapter 8:

The Final Move

Briony sat in the center of the clearing, her legs crossed beneath her and her hands resting on the smooth surface of The Channel. The midday light barely penetrated the dense canopy of Črni Les, leaving the forest floor shrouded in a perpetual twilight. Duska sat beside her, his tail wrapped around his paws, his green eyes fixed on the shadows that seemed to writhe at the edges of the clearing.

Most importantly, Briony had brought the talisman that Ana had blessed for her the day before. It was a small carved piece of hawthorn wood, no bigger than Briony's thumb, shaped into the ancient symbol of protection, a circle with a cross through its center. Ana had worked on it for hours, carving intricate designs into its surface and speaking words of power over it, drawing on the knowledge of generations of midwives who had come before her.

For a moment, nothing happened. The forest remained silent, the air still. Then, slowly, the plank began to move beneath her fingers.

It drifted across the board with a deliberate, measured pace, pausing over symbols that Briony had come to recognize: the crescent moon for secrets, the flame for destruction, the spiral for binding. The movements were not random; they were purposeful, guided by a will that was not her own.

Briony's heart raced, but she forced herself to remain calm. She had to stay focused, had to keep her mind clear. She could not afford to let fear overwhelm her now.

The plank came to rest on a symbol she had not seen it choose before—a pair of hands, palms pressed together as if in prayer. Briony frowned, unsure of its meaning. Then, without warning, the Spirit Cards that lay beside the board began to flutter, as if blown by an invisible wind.

One card lifted into the air and drifted toward her, landing face-up on the moss beside her knee. Briony picked it up with trembling fingers and stared at the image.

It showed a woman standing in the center of a circle of flames, her hands raised above her head. Her face was twisted in agony, her mouth open in a silent scream. Around her, shadowy figures watched, their faces obscured but their postures conveying judgment and condemnation. At the bottom of the card, written in faded ink, were the words: **The Burning**.

Briony's breath caught in her throat. She had seen this card before, but never like this, never with such vivid clarity. The flames seemed to flicker and dance on the surface of the card, and the woman's eyes... They looked directly at Briony, pleading and accusing all at once.

"I know what they did to you," Briony whispered. "I know it was wrong."

The plank moved again, faster this time, darting from symbol to symbol in a chaotic pattern that made Briony's head spin. The air around her grew colder, and the shadows at the edges of the clearing seemed to press inward, closing the space around her like a noose.

Another card rose into the air, a Lore and Legends Card this time. It landed beside the first, and Briony picked it up. The image on this card showed a cradle, empty and overturned, surrounded by black handprints. The words beneath read: **The Innocent Taken**.

Briony's stomach twisted. Lila. The curse wanted Lila.

"No," she said firmly, setting the card down. "You can't have her. She's done nothing to you."

The plank spun wildly across the board, and the forest around her seemed to come alive with sound, whispers, low and urgent, layering over one another until they formed a cacophony of voices. Briony could not make out individual words, but the tone was unmistakable: anger, pain, desperation.

"I want to help you," Briony said, raising her voice to be heard over the whispers. "But you have to tell me what you need. What will it take to break this curse?"

The whispers stopped abruptly, leaving the clearing in suffocating silence. Then, slowly, the plank moved again. This time, it spelled out a single word, letter by letter: T-R-U-T-H.

Briony's mind raced. Truth. She had learned the truth about Elsbeth's death, about the injustice that had been done to her. But was that enough? What more was there to uncover?

Before she could voice her question, the world around her began to shift.

The clearing blurred and darkened, the trees melting into shadows. Briony tried to stand, but her body would not obey. She felt herself being pulled downward, sinking into the moss as if it were quicksand. Panic flared in her chest, but before she could cry out, the sensation stopped. The world shifted around Briony like smoke caught in the wind.

She stood in the center of Senčna Vas, but it was not the village she knew. The buildings were older, the cobblestones rougher, the air thick with the smell of wood smoke and fear. And everywhere, people were gathering.

A crowd filled the village square, their faces twisted with anxiety and suspicion. At the center stood a woman with her hands bound before her, Elsbeth Korrin.

But this wasn't an execution. Not yet. This was something else. This was a trial.

An elder stood on a raised platform, his voice booming across the square.

"Elsbeth Korrin! You are accused of witchcraft. Of consorting with dark forces. Of bringing sickness and death to our village!"

"No!" Elsbeth's voice was strong despite her bindings. "I have harmed no one! I am a healer, a midwife. I have saved your children, delivered your babies, tended your sick!"

But the crowd murmured, uncertain and afraid. Then a woman stepped forward from the throng, and Briony's breath caught in her throat.

She was older than Elsbeth, her face lined with age but still beautiful. In her arms, she carried a baby wrapped in a soft cloth. The infant slept peacefully, unaware of the horror unfolding around it.

"Lillith," Briony whispered.

Lillith's voice rang out clear and cold.

"I have seen her, brothers and sisters! I have seen Elsbeth with the forbidden tools. She carved symbols into wood, symbols to call the dead. She has opened doors that should remain closed!"

Elsbeth's face went white. "No, Lillith, please—you know that's not—"

"I found this in her cottage!" Lillith held up a wooden board carved with strange letters and symbols. The Channel. "She used it to speak with spirits, to disturb the boundary between life and death. This is why the darkness has come to us! This is why our crops fail and our animals sicken!"

The crowd erupted in angry shouts. Elsbeth stared at Lillith, betrayal and understanding dawning in her eyes.

"You," Elsbeth breathed. "You brought the darkness. You meddled with forces you didn't understand, and now you blame me to hide your own sins."

But her words were drowned out by the mob's fury. The elders conferred in hushed tones, their faces grave.

"Elsbeth Korrin," the head elder pronounced, "you are found guilty of witchcraft. You will be removed from this village and cast out into the wilderness. May God have mercy on your soul."

Cast out. The words echoed through the square. The villagers nodded, satisfied that justice had been served. They would never see Elsbeth again. She would be gone, and the curse would go with her.

But Briony could see the truth in the elders' eyes, in the way they avoided looking at each other. They had already decided on something worse than exile.

Then the vision shifted.

Now Briony stood in Črni Les, the Black Wood. The crowd was gone. The village was far off in the distance. Here, in a clearing where the trees grew so thick that even noon felt like twilight, five hooded figures stood in a circle.

At the center, bound to a post of blackened wood, stood Elsbeth Korrin. No trial now. No villagers to witness. Only the five elders who had lied to their people.

"You told them I would be exiled," Elsbeth said, her voice shaking not with fear but with rage. "You told them I would leave. But you brought me here to murder me."

The tallest elder stepped forward, a torch in his trembling hand. "You are too dangerous to live, Elsbeth Korrin. Exile is not enough. The village must be cleansed."

"Cleansed?" Elsbeth laughed, bitter and broken. "You burn an innocent woman to hide another's guilt! Lillith opened the door to darkness, and I am your sacrifice to close it again!"

"The decision is made," the elder said coldly.

Briony wanted to scream, to run forward, to stop them, but she was frozen, forced to witness what had happened three centuries ago.

The torches lowered. The kindling caught. Flames rushed upward, hungry and merciless. And as the fire consumed her, Elsbeth's screams tore through the forest, screams that would echo across generations.

"I curse you!" Her voice rose above the crackling flames. "I curse this village! I curse the lies you tell! My hands, hands that healed and delivered and saved, let them mark you! Let them appear as proof of your crime! Let no one forget what you did here in secret!"

The elders stood in their circle and watched until the screaming stopped. When they returned to the village at dawn, they told the people that Elsbeth had been cast out. That she had cursed them as she left. That her evil words might linger, but she herself was gone.

The village believed the lie. Only five men knew the truth—that an innocent woman had burned in the Black Wood while her betrayer slept peacefully with a baby in her arms.

The vision released Briony suddenly, and she gasped, falling forward onto her hands and knees.

"Two crimes," she whispered, understanding flooding through her. "They didn't just murder you. They lied about it. The whole village thinks you were exiled. They don't know you were burned alive. They don't know the elders are murderers."

Elsbeth's presence wrapped around her like cold mist.

"They hid the truth. Buried it in the forest where no one would find it. The confession you carry proves the murder—but the village still believes the lie. And Lillith... Lillith became a hero. They praised her for exposing me. She built her reputation on my ashes and raised her daughter on my stolen legacy."

Briony pulled out the confession letter, holding it up to the darkness. "Then I'll tell them. I'll show them what really happened. I'll expose the truth of Lillith's betrayal and the elders' murder. The whole truth."

"Will they listen?" Elsbeth's voice was sad now, weary. "Or will they call you mad? Will they burn you too, to keep their comfortable lies intact?"

Briony's hands tightened on the letter. "I don't know. But I have to try. For you. For Lila. For every midwife who's suffered because of this curse."

Chapter 9:

The Choice

Briony stumbled out of the clearing, her legs unsteady and her mind still reeling from what she had witnessed through The Channel. The vision of Elsbeth's trial in the village square, the crowd's fear, Lillith's betrayal, the public condemnation, all played over and over in her head like a nightmare she could not escape. And then the second vision, the darker truth: the secret execution in Črni Les, where only five hooded elders stood witness as Elsbeth burned and cursed them all.

The revelation of Lillith's betrayal cut deeper still. To know that an elder midwife, a woman who was supposed to protect life, had orchestrated such a monstrous act to hide her own crimes... It shook the very foundation of everything Briony believed about her calling.

The weight of the truth she now carried pressed down on her like a boulder threatening to crush her beneath its weight. Every step felt labored, as if she were wading through deep water. Her hands were still trembling from touching The Channel, and she could not shake the lingering sensation of Elsbeth's presence, that terrible mix of anger and sorrow that seemed to have seeped into Briony's very bones.

Duska trotted ahead of her on the narrow forest path, his dark form moving with sure-footed confidence through the shadows. He stopped occasionally to glance back, his green eyes bright in the gloom, making sure she was following. The cat's presence was a small comfort, a reminder that she was not entirely alone, even here in the depths of Črni Les, where the shadows seemed to have a life of their own and the air itself felt heavy with ancient malice.

The walk back to Ana's house felt longer than usual, each step an effort. Briony's thoughts churned endlessly, circling the same questions over and over. She had the confession letter from Tomás, proof that the elders had murdered Elsbeth in the forest. But the letter said nothing about Lillith, nothing about who had truly set the tragedy in motion. And even if she could prove Lillith's role, would it be enough to break the curse? Or would Elsbeth's anger demand something more, something Briony was not willing to give?

By the time she reached Ana's door, the sun had begun its descent toward the horizon, painting the sky in shades of amber and crimson. Briony knocked, and within moments, the door swung open to reveal Ana's worried face.

"Thank the heavens," Ana breathed, pulling Briony inside. "I've been watching for you all day. When you didn't return by midafternoon, I thought..." She stopped herself, shaking her head. "Never mind. You're here now. That's what matters."

Marko appeared from the back room, Lila cradled in his arms. The baby was awake and content, her small fist wrapped around one of Marko's fingers. When she saw Briony, her face lit up with recognition, and she let out a delighted coo.

Briony's heart swelled with love and relief. She crossed the room and took Lila from Marko's arms, holding her daughter close and breathing in her sweet scent.

"She's been good," Marko said with a gentle smile. "Fussed a bit around noon, but Ana sang to her, and she settled right down."

"Thank you," Briony whispered, her voice thick with emotion. "Both of you. I don't know what I'd do without you."

Ana placed a hand on Briony's shoulder. "You don't have to thank us. Now, come sit. You look exhausted. Tell us what happened."

Briony sank into a chair by the fire, Lila nestled in her lap. Duska jumped up onto the armrest and curled into a ball, purring softly. For a moment, Briony simply sat there, absorbing the warmth and safety of Ana's home. Then, slowly, she began to speak.

She told them everything, about returning to The Channel, about the cards and symbols that had appeared, about the visions Elsbeth had shown her. She described the two scenes: first, the public trial in the village square where Lillith had accused Elsbeth before the gathered crowd, holding up The Channel itself as evidence of witchcraft. Then the second, darker vision of the five elders taking Elsbeth into the Black Wood under the pretense of exile, and burning her there in secret, where no villagers would witness their crime.

"The village was told she was exiled," Briony said, her voice heavy with the weight of the revelation. "They watched the elders lead her away and believed she was simply being cast out. But it was a lie. The elders took her into Črni Les and murdered her there. Only the five of them knew the truth. The rest of the village has believed for three hundred years that Elsbeth cursed them as she left. They don't know she was burned alive. They don't know the elders are murderers."

Ana and Marko listened in silence, their expressions growing more troubled with each word.

"Lillith," Ana murmured when Briony finished. "I've heard that name before. She's part of the village's history, praised for her skill and wisdom. But if what you're saying is true..."

"It is true," Briony said firmly. "I saw it. Elsbeth showed me. Lillith had dabbled in forbidden magic, summoned something dark that she couldn't control. She needed someone to blame, someone to sacrifice to seal away the darkness she'd called forth. So she accused Elsbeth, her friend, a woman who had tried to help her. She gave the elders The Channel as evidence and watched as they dragged Elsbeth away. And when Elsbeth burned in the forest, Lillith was safe in the village, her crimes hidden, her reputation intact."

Briony reached into her dress and pulled out the folded parchment, the confession letter she had retrieved from the chapel. She spread it carefully on the table between them. "I have this. Tomás's confession. It proves the elders murdered Elsbeth in the forest. It says she was innocent. But..."

"But it doesn't mention Lillith," Ana said softly, scanning the aged handwriting.

"No." Briony's voice was heavy with frustration. "Tomás writes about their guilt, about knowing Elsbeth was innocent, about the horror of what they did. But he never names who accused her or why. He may not have known about Lillith's role. She manipulated them, fed them lies, gave them evidence. They thought they were protecting the village from a witch."

"So even with this confession, we can't prove Lillith's guilt," Marko said, his face grave.

"And even if we could," Ana added slowly, "would it be enough? The confession tells us what happened, but curses don't break just because the truth is revealed. Elsbeth's spirit has been bound to this village for centuries. Her pain, her rage, it's deeper than words on paper."

Briony felt tears burning in her eyes. "Then what good is it? What good is proof if it can't save Lila?"

"It's important," Ana said firmly, taking Briony's hand. "The letter validates what we suspected. It's a weapon against the lies that have sustained the curse. But you're right, it's not enough by itself. The curse feeds on injustice, yes, but it also feeds on Elsbeth's unresolved spirit. We need to understand what she truly wants, what will allow her to finally rest."

"There may be other records," Ana continued thoughtfully. "Documents from that time in the chapel's archives, birth records, death records, accusations. If Lillith truly did what Elsbeth claims, there may be some trace of it. Some record of her acquiring forbidden knowledge, or of events that preceded Elsbeth's trial. I could search for them, discreetly. I'm still trusted in the village."

"But even if we find such records," Marko interjected, his voice heavy, "even if we expose Lillith's crimes three hundred years later, will that break the curse? She's long dead. Her descendants are respected members of the village. Elsbeth's spirit won't rest just because we know the truth. She wants more than acknowledgment."

Briony stared at the confession in Ana's hands, feeling the weight of those old words. "She wants justice. Real justice. Not just for the elders who burned her, but for Lillith who betrayed her. And I fear..." Her voice dropped to a whisper. "I fear she thinks the only justice is the same sacrifice that created the curse, a midwife and her child."

Ana's face went pale. "No. Briony, you cannot..."

"I won't," Briony said firmly, though her hands were shaking. "I won't give her Lila. I won't continue the cycle of sacrifice. There has to be another way." She looked down at the confession in Ana's hands, then back up at her mentor. "The letter proves Elsbeth was murdered. Now I need to find out how to free her without becoming her next victim."

Briony carefully folded the confession and tucked it back into her dress, feeling the parchment's weight against her heart. "I have to go back to The Channel," she said quietly. "I have to speak with Elsbeth directly. I have to find out what she needs, not just acknowledgment of the truth, but justice. Real justice that doesn't demand more innocent blood."

Ana looked toward the forest in the distance, toward the dark line of trees that marked the edge of Črni Les. "Then rest tonight. Gather your strength. When you're ready, I'll watch over Lila. And Briony..." Ana's eyes were fierce. "You come back. You hear me? Whatever Elsbeth demands, you find another way. You come back to your daughter."

"I will," Briony promised, holding Lila tighter. "I will."

The next evening, as the light faded and the village settled into uneasy sleep, Briony found herself standing at the edge of Črni Les once more. She had left Lila with Ana and Marko again, trusting them to keep her daughter safe. In her hands, she carried the talisman Ana had blessed, along with a small bundle of protective herbs. And tucked inside her dress, pressed against her heart, was the confession letter, proof of murder, even if it wasn't the whole truth.

The forest was darker than ever, the mist thick and cloying. Briony could barely see the path ahead of her, but Duska moved confidently through the shadows, his dark form a guiding presence.

When they reached the clearing, Briony stopped at its edge and stared. The space looked different now, charged with an energy that made the hairs on the back of her neck stand on end. The air shimmered faintly, as if the boundary between the world of the living and the world of spirits had grown thin.

Briony stepped into the clearing and knelt beside The Channel. She did not uncover it this time; she did not need to. She could feel its presence beneath the moss and leaves, pulsing like a heartbeat.

"Elsbeth," she called out, her voice steady despite the fear coiling in her gut like a living serpent. "I need to speak with you. I need to understand what you truly want from me. Please. Show yourself."

For a moment, there was only silence, a silence so complete and absolute that it felt like the world itself had stopped breathing. Even Duska went still, his ears pricked forward, his body tense and ready to flee.

Then the air in the clearing began to change. The temperature dropped so rapidly that Briony could see her breath misting in front of her face in great white clouds. Frost began to form on the moss at her feet, spreading outward in delicate crystalline patterns. The shadows at the edges of the clearing began to shift and move, detaching themselves from the trees and flowing toward the center like smoke drawn by an invisible wind.

Briony's fingers tightened around the talisman at her neck, feeling its warmth pulse against her palm, a small beacon of light in the gathering darkness.

And then Elsbeth appeared.

The spirit manifested before her, more solid and substantial than she had ever been. Her form was no longer translucent or flickering but seemed almost corporeal, as if she had stepped out of the past and into the present. She looked exactly as she had in the visions, a woman in her middle or late thirties, with dark hair that hung loose around her pale face in tangled waves. She wore a simple dress, faded and worn, the kind that a midwife might have worn centuries ago.

But it was her eyes that captured Briony's attention, those deep, sorrowful eyes that seemed to hold within them an ocean of pain and anger. They were fixed on Briony with an intensity that made her shiver, boring into her as if Elsbeth could see straight through to her soul.

And her hands. Dear God, her hands.

They hung at her sides, blackened and charred, the skin peeling away in places to reveal the white bone and gray ash beneath. They were the hands of someone who had burned alive, someone who had died in unimaginable agony. The sight of them made Briony's stomach turn, but she forced herself not to look away. This was Elsbeth's truth. This was what had been done to her.

"You called," Elsbeth said, her voice soft but carrying an undercurrent of power. "Why?"

Briony took a deep breath, forcing herself to meet the spirit's gaze. "I want to help you. I want to break this curse. But I need to know, what do you really want from me? Is exposing Lillith's crimes truly enough? I have proof of the elders' murder, but not of her betrayal."

She pulled the confession from her dress and held it up. "The elder Tomás wrote this. He admits they burned you in the forest, that you were innocent. But he doesn't name Lillith. He may not have known what she did."

Elsbeth's gaze lingered on the old parchment, something flickering in her expression, recognition, perhaps, or a bitter satisfaction.

"You found his words," Elsbeth said softly. "He was the only one who felt true remorse. The only one who tried, in his cowardly way, to make amends." She paused. "But you already know the answer to your question, Briony. You've known since the moment you touched The Channel. A confession written three hundred years ago cannot undo what was done. It cannot break the chains that bind me here."

Briony's heart sank. "Then tell me. What will?"

Elsbeth took a step closer, and the temperature in the clearing dropped even further. "The curse was born from betrayal and sacrifice. Lillith offered me to the flames to bind the darkness she had summoned. She gave them an innocent woman and her unborn child. And so the curse demands the same, a midwife and her newborn child, offered to the shadows."

"No," Briony whispered, shaking her head. "No, there has to be another way."

"There is no other way," Elsbeth said, her voice hardening. "That is the nature of curses, Briony. They do not forgive. They do not forget. They feed on suffering, and they demand payment."

"But I've done nothing wrong!" Briony cried, her voice breaking. "Lila has done nothing wrong! Why should we have to pay for Lillith's sins?"

"Because that is how the cycle continues," Elsbeth replied, her tone almost pitying. "Do you think I wanted this? Do you think I chose to bind my spirit to this place, to haunt the village for centuries? I did not. But Lillith's betrayal set this in motion, and it will not end until the debt is paid."

Briony's mind raced. She thought of Lila, sleeping peacefully in Ana's arms, unaware of the danger that surrounded her. She thought of all the midwives who had come before her, all the babies who had been lost to the curse. And she thought of herself, young, afraid, but determined to protect the one thing that mattered most.

"I won't do it," Briony said, her voice firm. "I won't give you my daughter. And I won't offer myself to your curse. There has to be another way, and I will find it."

Elsbeth's expression darkened, and the shadows around her seemed to grow deeper, more oppressive. "You cannot fight this, Briony. The curse is too strong. If you refuse, it will take what it wants anyway. You will watch your daughter suffer, and then it will come for you. And when it does, there will be no mercy."

"Then I'll break the curse myself," Briony said, her hands clenching into fists. "I'll find a way to sever the connection between you and this place. I'll free you whether you want it or not."

For a long moment, Elsbeth said nothing. She simply stared at Briony, her expression unreadable. Then, slowly, she smiled, a sad, bitter smile that held no warmth.

"You are brave," Elsbeth said softly. "Braver than I was. But bravery will not save you. Only sacrifice can do that."

"I don't believe that," Briony replied. "And I won't give up."

Elsbeth's smile faded, and her form began to flicker, growing less solid. "Then make your choice, Briony. Accept the curse and spare the village further suffering, or refuse and watch as everything you love is destroyed."

"I choose neither," Briony said, her voice ringing out clear and strong in the cold air. "I refuse both paths. I choose to fight. I choose to break this curse without sacrificing anyone, not myself, not my daughter, not anyone else. There has to be another way, and I will find it."

For a long moment, Elsbeth simply stared at her, her expression unreadable. Then, slowly, her lips curved into a smile, but it was not a warm smile. It was sad and bitter, the smile of someone who has heard brave words before and watched them crumble into dust.

"You have the truth in your hands," Elsbeth said, gesturing to the confession letter. "But truth alone cannot free me. I am bound by something far stronger than lies. I am bound by magic, by blood, by the very tool Lillith used to summon the darkness. Until that anchor is destroyed, I will never be free. And neither will you."

"What anchor?" Briony demanded. "Tell me!"

But Elsbeth's form was already fading. "You already know," the spirit whispered. "It is beneath your hands even now."

Briony looked down at The Channel, realization dawning like cold fire in her chest.

Elsbeth's laughter echoed through the clearing, a hollow, mournful sound that seemed to come from everywhere at once. It was the laugh of someone who had lost everything, who had suffered beyond measure, and who no longer believed in hope or redemption.

"So be it," the spirit said, her voice layered with sadness and a terrible resignation. "You are brave, Briony. Perhaps too brave for your own good. But bravery alone will not save you. Know this: The darkness that Lillith summoned is still here, waiting in the spaces between worlds. It has patience. It has time. And it will not stop until it has what it wants. It will hunt you. It will haunt your dreams. It will turn the village against you. And when you are weakest, when you have nothing left, it will take what it desires."

Briony opened her mouth to respond, to argue, but Elsbeth raised one blackened hand to silence her.

"You have made your choice," Elsbeth said. "Now face the consequences."

With that, Elsbeth's form began to dissolve, her body breaking apart into tendrils of mist caught by an invisible wind and scattered across the clearing. Within seconds, she was gone, leaving Briony alone in the oppressive silence once more.

For a long moment, Briony simply knelt there on the cold moss, her heart pounding so hard she thought it might burst from her chest. Her mind raced, trying to process everything that had just happened. The Channel. It was The Channel, the tool Elsbeth had created to communicate with the husband she missed so desperately, the bridge between worlds that anchored the curse to this place.

If she destroyed it, would the curse break?

She had made her choice. She would not sacrifice herself or Lila. She would find another way to break the curse, even if it meant standing alone against the darkness, even if the entire village turned against her.

But as she rose to her feet and turned to leave the clearing, her legs shaky and weak beneath her, a sound stopped her in her tracks.

A low, guttural growl came from the shadows at the edge of the clearing.

It was unlike any sound she had ever heard, deeper than an animal's growl, more resonant, vibrating through the air and into her chest. It made her teeth ache and her skin crawl with primal fear.

Briony spun around, her heart leaping into her throat, her breath coming in short, panicked gasps. Duska's fur stood on end, making him look twice his normal size. He let out a warning hiss, his back arched, his eyes fixed on something at the edge of the clearing that Briony could not quite see.

The shadows there were moving, not drifting or swaying like normal shadows, but moving with purpose and intent. They were gathering, coalescing, forming into something solid and terrible.

And from within them, something began to emerge.

It was not Elsbeth. It was not human. It was something far older and far more dangerous, a manifestation of the curse itself, the darkness that Lillith had summoned centuries ago and bound to this place with blood and fire and sacrifice.

It had no clear form, no defined edges. It was simply darkness given shape and will, a roiling, churning mass of shadow and cold and malevolence. Briony could feel its hunger radiating outward like heat from a furnace, could sense its ancient rage and its insatiable need to feed.

Briony stumbled backward, her hand flying to the talisman at her neck. She clutched it with desperate fingers, feeling its warmth pulse against her palm, a faint protection against the darkness that now threatened to consume her.

"Stay back," she whispered, her voice shaking but defiant. "Stay back! You have no power over me!"

But the darkness did not listen. It moved closer, flowing across the ground like oil, pressing in from all sides. The air grew colder still, and Briony's breath came out in ragged white clouds. She could feel the curse trying to wrap itself around her, trying to find a way in, searching for weakness.

And Briony realized with a sinking sense of dread that she was out of time. She had challenged the curse, had refused its demand for sacrifice, and now it was coming for her.

The curse had made its move. And now, it was her turn to respond, to fight or flee, to stand her ground or be consumed.

She tightened her grip on the talisman and whispered a prayer to whatever gods or spirits might be listening.

"Please," she breathed. "Help me. I can't do this alone."

And somewhere, in the back of her mind, a voice whispered: *The Channel. Destroy The Channel.*

Chapter 10:

Breaking the Curse

The darkness surged forward like a living thing, cold and hungry and ancient, pressing against Briony from all sides with suffocating force. It was not simply the absence of light; it was a presence unto itself, malevolent and aware, moving with terrible purpose. She could feel it probing at the edges of her consciousness, seeking weakness, seeking any crack in her defenses through which it might slip and take control.

Her breath came in short, panicked gasps that burned in her lungs. The air had grown so cold that each inhale felt like swallowing shards of ice. Her fingers tightened around the talisman at her neck until her knuckles turned white and her nails dug into her palms hard enough to draw blood. The small piece of carved hawthorn wood was warm, almost hot, against her skin, pulsing with energy that pushed back against the darkness, but it felt so small compared to the vastness of what she faced.

"No," she whispered, her voice barely audible over the rushing sound in her ears, a sound like wind or water or the whispers of a thousand angry spirits all speaking at once. "You won't have me. You won't have Lila. I won't let you."

The shadows coiled tighter around her, wrapping around her arms and legs like invisible chains, constricting her movement and pulling her down. Briony felt her knees begin to buckle under the sheer weight of the curse's pressure. It was immense, far greater than she had imagined, a crushing force that seemed to press down on her from above and squeeze inward from all sides simultaneously.

She realized with horrified clarity that this was not just Elsbeth's anger she faced now. This was something far larger, far older. It was the accumulated darkness of centuries, all the fear and superstition and violence that had fed the curse since Lillith first summoned it in her moment of desperation and cowardice. Every wrongful accusation, every act of cruelty, every innocent life taken by fear-maddened mobs... All of it had poured into this curse, making it stronger, giving it substance and power.

Duska let out a sharp, piercing yowl and launched himself at the shadows. The cat's small body collided with the darkness, and for a brief moment, the pressure around Briony eased. Duska hissed and clawed at something Briony could not see, his fur standing on end, his eyes wild with protective fury.

"Duska!" Briony cried out, stumbling forward. But the cat did not retreat. He fought with a ferocity that seemed impossible for such a small creature, buying Briony precious seconds to gather her thoughts.

The talisman. Ana had blessed it specifically for this purpose, to protect against dark magic, to shield the wearer from supernatural harm. But Briony had not yet activated it, had not yet spoken the words of the protection spell.

With trembling hands, she pulled the talisman from around her neck and held it before her. The small piece of carved hawthorn wood felt warm in her palm, pulsing with a gentle energy that stood in stark contrast to the cold malevolence surrounding her.

"By the blood of midwives past," Briony began, her voice shaking but growing stronger with each word. "By innocence betrayed, by light against shadow, "

The darkness recoiled, as if the words themselves were weapons. Briony felt a surge of hope and pressed on, raising her voice.

"I call upon the power of healing, the strength of those who bring life into this world. I call upon justice and truth, upon love and protection. I break the chains that bind this curse to the innocent. I sever the connection between past and present, between anger and vengeance!"

The talisman began to glow, faintly at first, then brighter, until it shone like a small sun in Briony's hand. The light spread outward in waves, pushing back the shadows that had surrounded her. Duska darted back to her side, his fur singed but his spirit unbroken.

The darkness let out a sound like a scream, high-pitched and inhuman, and retreated to the edges of the clearing. But it did not disappear entirely. It gathered there, watching, waiting.

And then Elsbeth appeared once more.

The spirit stood at the center of the clearing, her form flickering between solid and translucent. Her expression was no longer angry or vengeful; it was something far more complex. Pain, sorrow, longing, and a desperate, aching hope.

"You would fight for your child," Elsbeth said, her voice soft and distant, as if she were speaking from a great distance or from across the barrier between life and death. There was something different in her tone now. The anger had not disappeared entirely, but it had been joined by something else. Understanding, perhaps. Or recognition. "As I would have fought for mine, had I been given the chance."

Briony's breath caught in her throat, her heart clenching painfully in her chest. "You had a child?"

Elsbeth nodded slowly, her blackened hands rising to press against her chest, over the place where her heart had once beat. When she spoke again, her voice was thick with a grief so profound that it seemed to fill the entire clearing, seeping into the ground and the trees and the very air itself.

"A daughter," Elsbeth said, and Briony could hear the love and longing in those two simple words. "I was carrying her when they accused me, when Lillith stood before the village and held up The Channel as proof of my witchcraft. When the elders dragged me away under the pretense of exile. I was five months along. I could feel her moving inside me, feel her little kicks and turns. I used to talk to her in the darkness, tell her stories, promise her that everything would be alright."

Elsbeth's form flickered, becoming less solid for a moment, as if the memory was too painful to sustain her manifestation. "The village thought I was being exiled. They watched the elders lead me away, believing I would simply disappear into the wilderness. They didn't know the truth, that the elders were taking me to Črni Les to murder me in secret, where no witnesses would see their crime."

The spirit's voice hardened, turning bitter and cold. "Lillith knew I was pregnant. She had been the one to confirm it, had examined me herself, and told me with a smile that I was going to be a mother. She had seemed happy for me. I thought she was my friend. But when the darkness she summoned threatened to consume her, when she needed someone to blame and someone to sacrifice, she said nothing about my pregnancy. She stood in the village square and accused me of consorting with evil. She provided the evidence. She watched as they led me away."

Briony felt tears streaming down her cheeks. "I'm so sorry, Elsbeth."

"They burned me in the forest," Elsbeth continued, her voice breaking. "Only the five elders were there to witness. And when the flames consumed me, when I screamed not for myself but for my unborn daughter, there was no one to hear except my murderers. My little girl never got to take a single breath, never got to see the sun or feel the rain or know that she was loved."

The full horror of what had been done to Elsbeth crashed over Briony like a wave, threatening to drag her under with its terrible weight. It was not just an innocent woman who had been murdered—it was a mother and her unborn child, two lives snuffed out to cover up another's crimes. And the village didn't even know. They thought Elsbeth had been exiled, cursed them, and left.

"I'm so sorry," Briony whispered again, her voice breaking with emotion. "Elsbeth, what they did to you, what she did to you, it was monstrous. It was unforgivable. You and your daughter deserved so much better. You deserved to live. You deserved to be happy."

"Sorry does not bring back the dead," Elsbeth replied, but her voice was gentler now, less harsh. "Sorry does not undo the pain. But perhaps... perhaps it is a beginning."

The darkness at the edges of the clearing began to stir again, and Briony could feel its hunger intensifying. It did not care about apologies or understanding. It only cared about feeding, about perpetuating the cycle of suffering that had sustained it for so long.

"The curse will not release you easily," Elsbeth said, her gaze shifting to the shadows. "Lillith's spell was powerful, fueled by the darkest of magic. The Channel, the tool I so foolishly created, became the anchor when I died. My spirit bound itself to it in my final moments, using it as a bridge to reach back into the world of the living. As long as it exists, the curse will endure."

Briony looked down at the ground where The Channel lay hidden beneath moss and leaves. "Then I'll destroy it," she said, her voice steady with newfound determination. "I'll break the anchor and free you."

"But know this," Elsbeth warned, her voice grave. "Destroying The Channel will not be without cost. The relic has absorbed centuries of dark energy. When it is broken, that energy will be released all at once. You must be strong enough to withstand it, or it will consume you."

Briony looked down at the talisman in her hand, still glowing with soft, warm light. Ana had blessed it with all the power and knowledge of generations of midwives. If anything could protect her, it would be this.

"I can do it," Briony said, her voice steady. "I have to. For Lila. For you. For every woman who's suffered because of this curse."

She pulled the confession letter from her dress and held it up. "I have proof of what the elders did to you. Tomás wrote it down, his guilt, his confession. It doesn't name Lillith, but it proves you were murdered in the forest, that you were innocent. When this is over, I'll make sure the village knows the truth. I'll clear your name. Your suffering won't be forgotten."

Elsbeth's expression softened as she looked at the old parchment. "You found Tomás's words. Keep them. Share the truth when the village is ready to hear it. Clear my name, not for vengeance, but so that no other midwife suffers what

I and so many have suffered. So that the lies that sustained this curse are finally exposed."

"I will," Briony promised. "I swear it."

Elsbeth's form began to grow fainter. "Then do it now, before the darkness regains its strength. And Briony... thank you. For seeing me not as a monster, but as what I truly am: a mother who wanted only to protect her child."

With those words, Elsbeth vanished, leaving Briony alone with Duska and the churning shadows.

Briony dropped to her knees and began to brush away the moss and leaves that covered The Channel. The dark wood was cold beneath her fingers, the symbols carved into its surface seeming to writhe and shift in the dim light. She could feel the power radiating from it, ancient and malevolent, and her stomach twisted with fear.

But she did not hesitate. She could not afford to.

"By the light of truth and the strength of love," Briony said, her voice ringing out clear and strong, "I cast you out. I break the chains that bind you. I destroy the bridge between worlds."

She raised the talisman high above her head and brought it down with all her strength, striking the center of The Channel.

The wood splintered with a sound like thunder, and a shockwave of energy exploded outward from the relic. Briony was thrown backward, the force of the blast knocking the breath from her lungs. The talisman flew from her hand and landed in the moss several feet away, its light flickering but not extinguished.

The shadows screamed, a terrible, keening wail that seemed to come from everywhere at once. They surged forward, converging on the broken pieces of The Channel, trying desperately to hold onto the anchor that had sustained them for so long.

But it was too late. The relic was shattered, its power bleeding away into the earth. The symbols on the wood glowed bright red, then faded to dull gray. The air itself seemed to crack and tear, releasing centuries of trapped energy in a violent rush.

Briony struggled to her feet, her body aching and her vision blurred. She could see the shadows writhing and twisting, growing less substantial with each passing moment. They clawed at the air, reaching for her, but their forms were dissolving, breaking apart like smoke in the wind.

And then, in the center of the clearing, Elsbeth appeared one final time.

The spirit looked different now, younger, more vibrant. Her hair was no longer tangled and matted but fell in soft waves around her face. Her hands were no longer blackened and burned but smooth and whole. And her expression was... peaceful. Content.

Beside her, barely visible but undeniably present, was the faint outline of a small child, a daughter who had never been born, now reunited with her mother at last.

"You did it," Elsbeth said, her voice filled with wonder. "You broke the curse."

Briony nodded, too exhausted to speak.

"I am free," Elsbeth continued, her form beginning to glow with a soft, golden light. "And so is my daughter. We can finally rest."

"I'm glad," Briony managed to say, her voice hoarse. "You deserve peace."

Elsbeth smiled, a true, genuine smile that transformed her face. "And so do you. You are stronger than you know, Briony. You faced the darkness and did not flinch. You chose love over fear, truth over lies. That is true courage."

"I'll keep my promise," Briony said, touching the confession letter still tucked in her dress. "I'll tell them what really happened. I'll make sure your name is cleared."

"And Lillith?" Elsbeth asked, her voice carefully neutral.

Briony's jaw tightened. "She's dead. She's been dead for centuries. I can't punish her. But I can make sure her crime isn't forgotten. That her legacy isn't one of honor and respect built on your ashes. The village will know the truth, all of it."

Elsbeth was silent for a long moment. Then, slowly, she nodded. "That is enough. Truth, even truth spoken centuries late, has power. The curse was born from lies and buried secrets. You have brought those secrets into the light. That is the justice I needed, not blood, not sacrifice, but truth."

Elsbeth's form grew brighter, the golden light enveloping her and the small child beside her completely. "Go to your daughter. Hold her close. Live your life without fear. And remember, you are not alone. The spirits of the midwives who came before you, who fought and suffered and endured, they walk with you always."

And with that, Elsbeth was gone, not vanished into shadow or mist, but lifted upward, toward the light. Briony watched until the glow faded completely, leaving the clearing silent and still.

The shadows were gone. The oppressive weight that had hung over the forest was lifted. Even the air felt lighter, cleaner, as if a long-held breath had finally been released.

Duska padded over to Briony and rubbed against her legs, purring softly. Briony reached down and scooped him into her arms, holding him close.

"We did it," she whispered into his fur. "It's over."

By the time Briony made her way back to Ana's house, dawn was breaking over Senčna Vas. The sky was painted in shades of pink and gold, and the mist that usually clung to the village had lifted, revealing the rooftops and chimneys in crisp detail.

As she walked through the streets, Briony noticed changes everywhere. The blackened crops in the gardens had begun to green again, new shoots pushing up through the soil. The river that ran along the edge of the village, which had been murky and foul-smelling for weeks, now ran clear and bright. Even the air smelled fresher, cleaner, as if a storm had passed and washed everything clean.

The villagers who were awake and moving about stopped to stare at her as she passed. Their expressions were wary, uncertain, but no longer openly hostile. Something had shifted, and though they did not yet understand what, they could feel it.

When Briony reached Ana's door, she knocked softly. The door swung open almost immediately, and Ana stood there, her eyes red-rimmed and tired but filled with relief.

"Briony," Ana breathed, pulling her inside. "Thank the heavens. I felt... something. A shift. I knew you had succeeded."

Briony nodded, pulling out the confession letter and holding it up. "It's done. The curse is broken. Elsbeth is at peace. And I have proof of what happened, proof that needs to be shared."

Marko appeared from the back room, Lila cradled in his arms. When the baby saw her mother, she let out a delighted squeal and reached out with her small hands.

Briony took her daughter and held her close, breathing in her sweet scent and feeling the warmth of her small body pressed against her chest. Tears streamed down Briony's face, tears of relief, of exhaustion, of overwhelming love.

"It's over," she whispered. "The curse is broken. Elsbeth is at peace. And now... now we tell the truth."

***

Three days later, Briony stood in the village square with Ana and Marko beside her. The confession of Tomás lay on a table before the gathered villagers, displayed for all to see. Beside it, Ana had placed documents she'd found in the chapel archives, records of Lillith acquiring forbidden texts, accusations that had been mysteriously dropped, and dates that aligned with Elsbeth's trial.

The crowd was wary, suspicious. They had suffered under the curse for weeks, and many still blamed Briony for bringing it upon them. But they had also seen the change, the handprints fading, the crops recovering, the livestock healing. Something had shifted, and they wanted to understand what.

"This is a confession," Briony said, her voice steady despite her fear. "Written by Tomás, one of your elders, three hundred years ago. In it, he admits to murdering Elsbeth Korrin, the midwife you were told was exiled for witchcraft."

Murmurs rippled through the crowd. Someone shouted, "How do we know it's real?"

Ana stepped forward, her voice calm and authoritative. "I have verified the signature, the seal, the handwriting. It is genuine. And I have found other records in the chapel archives." She gestured to the documents. "Records that show Elsbeth was accused by another midwife, Lillith Dragomir, just weeks after Lillith herself was nearly exposed for acquiring forbidden magical texts."

The crowd grew quieter, uncertain now.

Briony continued, her voice growing stronger. "Lillith accused Elsbeth in order to hide her own crimes. She had dabbled in dark magic, summoned forces she couldn't control. She needed someone to sacrifice, someone to blame. So she betrayed her friend, provided false evidence, and watched as the elders took Elsbeth away."

She paused, letting the words sink in. "We were told Elsbeth was exiled. The truth is, she was murdered in secret in Črni Les, in the Black Wood. Only the five elders witnessed it. The rest of us have been lied to. And the curse we've suffered for generations was born from that injustice, from the lies that covered up her murder."

An old woman in the crowd spoke up, her voice quavering. "Lillith Dragomir is honored in our village. She trained generations of midwives. She saved countless lives."

"Yes," Ana said gently. "She did. She lived a long life doing good works, perhaps to atone for what she'd done. But her good deeds don't erase her crime. And as long as we honor her without acknowledging the truth, we dishonor Elsbeth's memory."

The village elder, a man named Stefan, stepped forward to examine the confession. He read it slowly, his face grave. When he finished, he looked up at the gathered crowd.

"This is real," he said quietly. "And if it is real, then we have been living a lie for three hundred years. Our ancestors covered up a murder, and we have repeated that lie, unknowingly, to our children and grandchildren."

He turned to Briony. "What would you have us do?"

Briony took a deep breath. "Remember Elsbeth Korrin as she truly was: a healer, a midwife, an innocent woman and mother-to-be who was betrayed. Remove Lillith's name from the places of honor. Teach the truth to your children. And never again let fear turn you into monsters willing to believe lies rather than face uncomfortable truths."

The crowd was silent for a long moment. Then, slowly, Stefan nodded.

"It will be done," he said. "The truth, however painful, must be told."

Briony felt a weight lift from her shoulders. It wasn't complete vindication, not yet. Trust would take time to rebuild. But it was a beginning.

In the days and weeks that followed, the village continued to heal. The livestock recovered, their strength returning. New lambs were born healthy and strong. The crops grew tall and green, the vegetables ripening on their vines. The illnesses that had plagued the villagers disappeared, and children's laughter once again filled the streets.

The handprints in Briony's cottage faded completely, leaving behind only clean, unmarked walls. The cold drafts vanished, and the cottage felt warm and safe once more.

The villagers, though still wary at first, began to soften. Some approached Briony hesitantly to offer thanks or apologies. Others simply nodded to her in passing, acknowledging her presence without hostility. It would take time for full trust to be restored, but it was a beginning.

The confession remained in the village archives, a testament to what had been hidden for too long. And beside it, Ana placed a new document, a full account of Lillith's betrayal, of Elsbeth's innocence, of the secret murder in the Black Wood, so that future generations would know the whole story.

Several weeks after the curse had been broken, Briony returned to the clearing in Črni Les one final time. She found that nature had already begun to reclaim the space. Moss had crept over the broken pieces of The Channel, covering the symbols with soft green carpet. Vines had wound around the fragments, pulling them slowly into the earth. And wildflowers had sprung up all around—bright yellow buttercups, delicate white daisies, purple violets that swayed in the breeze.

Briony stood in the center of the clearing and closed her eyes, listening to the sounds of the forest. Birds sang in the trees overhead, their voices sweet and clear. A gentle breeze rustled the leaves, carrying with it the scent of pine and wildflowers and fresh earth. Somewhere in the distance, she could hear the babble of a stream, its waters running clear and cold over smooth stones.

It was peaceful here now, truly peaceful, free of the oppressive weight and terrible presence that had hung over it for so long.

"Thank you, Elsbeth," Briony whispered into the quiet air. "Thank you for trusting me. Thank you for letting me help you. Rest well, you and your daughter. May you find the peace and happiness in death that you were denied in life."

For a moment, she thought she felt something, a warmth in the air, a gentle presence, like a hand resting briefly on her shoulder in gratitude and farewell. Then it was gone, and she was alone in the clearing with only the birds and the breeze for company.

Briony smiled, a real and genuine smile that reached her eyes and lightened her heart. She felt lighter than she had in months, as if an enormous burden had been lifted from her shoulders.

She turned and walked away from the clearing, Duska trotting at her heels, his tail held high with feline confidence. They made their way back through the forest, following the familiar path toward the village and toward home.

Briony was ready to return to the life that awaited her, a life filled with light and hope and the promise of a future no longer shadowed by the past. She would continue her apprenticeship with Ana, learning the skills and knowledge that had been passed down through generations of midwives. She would raise Lila to be strong and brave and kind. She would find her place in Senčna Vas, earning the trust and respect of her neighbors through her actions and her dedication.

And she would remember. She would remember Elsbeth and all the other women who had suffered under the weight of the curse, who had been blamed and feared and destroyed by superstition and hatred. She would make sure their stories were not forgotten, that their sacrifices were honored.

The confession letter remained safe in the chapel archives, and the truth had been spoken. Elsbeth Korrin's name had been cleared. Lillith's betrayal had been exposed. And the village, slowly but surely, was learning to live with the uncomfortable truth rather than comfortable lies.

Because Briony understood now, with a clarity that had been forged in fire and darkness and pain, that she was not just a midwife. She was a keeper of truth, a protector of the innocent, a woman who had looked into the face of evil and refused to flinch.

And that, she knew with absolute certainty, was enough.